MORTAL SHOWDOWN

By

NIK KRASNO

ISBN 978-0-9930827-7-1

If you are Quentin Tarantino, Guy Ritchie or an aspiring director interested in adapting this book into a movie, please, feel free to contact the author.

This is a work of fiction. Names, characters, businesses, organisations, countries, places, events and incidents either are the product of the authors' imagination or are used fictitiously. Any resemblance to actual persons, living or dead, corporations, organisations, entities, events, or locations is entirely coincidental. This book contains sexual themes, violence, objectionable language and behaviour. If you are UNDERAGE, easily offended, unable to discern the difference between fiction and reality, dislike the use of profanity, are uptight, or righteous to the point where reading this book may pose danger to your immortal soul, then you should immediately cease reading any further. The author accepts no responsibility for any thoughts you may form after reading this book. *Caveat emptor.*

PARENTAL ADVISORY: EXPLICIT CONTENT!

SERIES:
RISE OF AN OLIGARCH, The Way It Is: Book One, 2014
MORTAL SHOWDOWN, The Way It Is: Book 1½, 2015

Prologue

While investigating an assassination attempt on their boss and a series of hostile actions towards his corporations, Boris and David - the closest friends and associates of the Ukrainian oligarch Mikhail Vorotavich, discovered a conspiracy to break apart Ukraine, merging parts of his homeland with Russia, in the first move towards creating a new Soviet Union. A member of the Ukrainian Parliament, and head of a multinational corporation with billion-dollar interests in a multitude of industries that included oil, gas, steel, insurance, pharmaceuticals, transport, construction, security and arms, maybe Mikhail had too much money and influence for the old Soviet-era hard-liners that drew up the annexing plan. A fervent advocate of Ukraine joining the EU, was this the reason he was in the crosshairs of such dangerous opponents? Or were there more personal reasons behind recent events. Out of a coma, but in deep shit, Mikhail needs to act immediately to release his kidnapped brother.

Paradise Lost?

I took a long draw on the Cuban cigar, while my gaze swept the Caribbean Sea, so perfectly calm this night and shimmering in the moonlight. The tranquillity of the surroundings was in direct opposition to the thoughts that now filled my mind. The phone call was not completely unexpected, but the timing surprised me, to say the least. That my enemies moved so quickly was testament to their determination to deal with me. I didn't know how I became Public Enemy No.1, but I knew they would not cease in their efforts to get to me. I watched the smoke drift away on the tropical breeze and wondered if there was some symbolic connection with my hopes and dreams.

Barely a month had passed since a sniper's bullet nearly ended my life. As I lay in a coma in an exclusive medical centre on the outskirts of Tel Aviv, a second hit squad tried to take me out. Thankfully, my friend David had been given a heads-up by Mossad, so when the assassins arrived at Ben Gurion Airport, my security waited to greet them. It was a second lucky escape, and I knew I wouldn't likely escape a third time.

Safely spirited away to the Cayman Islands, the peaceful Caribbean hideaway gave me a chance to gather my thoughts and prepare for the brewing storm.

The phone call had been short and to the point. They had Sasha, my older brother, and if I didn't make it to Red Square in forty eight hours, then he would be executed.

I threw back the vodka and checked my watch for the umpteenth time. Slumped in my chair, the weight of recent events lay heavily on my shoulders. They had Sasha through *my* fault. I brought this on my family. It became clear that my shadowy opponents would not rest until I was dead.

Less than forty five hours remaining. Forty four and a quarter to be precise. My brother is the bait and I'm the fish.

I flipped open the dossier that Arthur had put together and studied it once more. During a drunken night with Boris, my right hand man, the Ukrainian minister of defence had claimed that the legendary Puppet Master wanted me dead. Taking into account the multiple attacks, cross border planning and top level professionals involved in recent actions, only someone at the Puppet Master's level could be behind such events. The amount of information gathered by Arthur and his security team was impressive, and painted a picture of a monster. A monster who ordered the bombing of my Moscow headquarters just two weeks previously with all my staff inside. Five dead, seventeen injured, and an entirely collapsed five storey building.

Arthur, my laconic chief of security, had written a concise account of both the Puppet Master's military and clandestine achievements, from his participation in the violent suppression of the Prague spring in 1968, being chief commander of the operation solidifying Castro's grip over Cuba in the seventies, called *Caribbean Joy*, his time as deputy and then Chief Commander of the Soviet Union's Afghanistan contingent and finally his rise up the chain of command of the Soviet KGB in the following decade. These were mostly known facts, but obviously the unknown parts were more interesting. Before all the official and commanding positions, the rumours were that as a young officer in Soviet military intelligence he had strangled prisoners with his bare hands, tortured, stabbed, electrocuted and wasted in every possible way over a hundred suspected and known enemies of the USSR abroad.

All our evidence suggested that the Puppet Master held Sasha, who was taken out of his office in broad daylight in Kiev by a group of paramilitaries, who neutralised Sasha's heavily armed and well trained security detail and then, we assumed, flew to Moscow or somewhere close by without passing through any passport or border control in Ukraine. Not many organisations in the world were capable of such an operation and even fewer had the audacity to attempt it.

After the mysterious caller had issued his command, I immediately phoned Arthur, who was outside checking up on security, too many times a day, if you ask me, and contemplating a counter attack. I relayed the message; now all I could do was waiting for Arthur to get back to me with a plan of action.

'How the fuck can I prevail against such a monster, who on top of his dubious personal achievements has the backing of the entire Russian special forces and agencies?' I mused out loud.

Within an hour, my phone started ringing, breaking the chain of thought. It was Arthur, according to the background noises and public announcements, calling from the airport.

"Thank fuck for that! Arthur, I have an idea...I want you to go to Moscow and wait for me there. I'll be with you in..."

"Huh? Are you crazy?" He interrupted. "Boss, you don't cross the Russian border, no matter what. Too dangerous. I'm on my way to Moscow already to start making enquiries. I'll put a plan together and call you back." Arthur said, and hung up, not even waiting for my response.

I agreed with him though, it was a bad idea formed in the heart rather than the head. My going to Moscow should be the last resort. There had to be a way. I unscrewed the cap on another bottle and continued studying the Puppet Master's CV. No, I couldn't wait until Arthur came up with something, as I gradually realised it would take him half a day to get to Moscow. Slowly, a better plan started to form. At first just an idea, but after speaking to my old friend Oleg I upgraded it to a 'plan' status. It wasn't perfect and I didn't have time for something superb, but it was better than jumping into the vipers nest. I picked up my military grade wireless communication device and called my pilot.

"Be ready for takeoff in thirty minutes. Make sure the tanks are full, I'll brief you on our destination when I see you."

I gulped down the vodka and closed my eyes for a second. Exhaling deeply, I rose and placed the empty glass on the side table.

"Let's do this."

Life is Full of Surprises

As the sun peaked over the horizon, the plane took off for its long journey across the Atlantic Ocean. As it gained altitude, I was granted a view that I couldn't get enough off: the emerald sea sparkling as if precious stones were inlaid on its surface, and the magnificent white sands of the Caribbean islands and shores. I hadn't fully left yet and I was already nostalgic. This was my beautiful nirvana where I'd built my impenetrable fortress, and I had been coerced to trade this safe paradise for some distant hell where I was all too vulnerable.

But I felt that self-pitying was inappropriate - I sat in a comfortable white leather armchair aboard an executive Gulfstream jet, while my brother was already in hell. And I was to blame. My elder brother, who took care of me for much of our childhood, striving to replace our father, was in captivity because some insane motherfucker wanted me dead. This wasn't right, and innocent bystanders like my brother, shouldn't be involved. But in our era, it seemed, no moral principles were practically implemented anymore, although some were still professed by worthless hypocritical politicians. I was desperate and I was miserable, but still determined to put things right.

11

I had just woken up from a three week long coma to the worst possible hangover. A month ago I was almost on top of the world, making my final preparations to secure my climb to the number one spot on the billionaires' list, and now I was under a multi-layered attack on each and every level: personal, business and family.

Each day I regretted that I woke up. Dead, asleep or mentally impaired I would be better off, as my waking seemed only to trigger further offensives. Until the phone call about Sasha, I thought that at least my family were safe, but now I knew there were no boundaries to this attack. I called Arthur, Boris, and my old friend Oleg, to tell them I was in the air. There was nothing more I could do except try and relax, and let the game play out in my mind like a chess game, where every possible variation of moves needs to be considered.

The time away from Europe had not been just about recuperation. There had been a brief visit to New York for a meeting with the CIA to discuss mutual interests, and the arrival of my mother-in-law in the Caymans, for an awkward but necessary conversation about the past. It was my oversight that I'd never enquired into who was my wife Masha's father for all these years, but now it wasn't just curiosity, it was essential.

A few months previously, I had tasked Boris with entertaining the Minister of Defence of Ukraine with the purpose of securing my company, Neplokho Defence as the intermediary for selling naval defence systems. During their drunken, debauched time at a private luxury resort, when I was still in a coma, the old drunkard had mumbled something about not wanting Boris' boss to be targeted. Not only that he said it was all the Puppet Master's doing, but how strange it was, when he had referred to me as his son-in-law. Drunken or not, you can't neglect the words of a man in such a position.

***

It wasn't an easy conversation. Masha's mother came all the way to the Cayman Islands because I insisted.

After giving Sara a few minutes to greet the grandchildren, I led her and Masha to our spacious living room, offering them the cosy sofas set around a low, Balinese-style dark wooden table. I switched the TV off, air-conditioning on, asked Jane, our maid to bring some fruits and a jar of water and told her to make sure we were not bothered afterwards. She hurried off to the kitchen and was back in minutes with the refreshments. Sara sat fidgeting, like she sensed something was up. Jane shut the glass sliding doors, immediately suppressing the sounds of the ocean and the circling seagulls outside the hermetically sealed bulletproof doors.

With Masha and Sara sat side by side, anyone would recognise that they were mother and daughter. The major difference besides the age was the general expression each exuded: while Masha's was of confidence and satisfaction, Sara's bore the signs of tragedy and pain. Attempting to broach the sensitive subject as gently as I could in order to avoid too many tears, I began.

"Sara, thanks for coming over. It's really crucial at this point. You probably have some idea of what is going on. Did Masha tell you?"

I didn't really expect Sara or Masha to answer. After Sara nodded I continued.

"Listen, this guy who chases us, is not Mother Teresa and I can guess that your memories aren't the sweetest, but we need to know what happened in the past, because it might help us to understand his modus operandi. That is, if this Puppet Master is really Masha's father. If you had some kind of relationship with him, it would be safe to assume that it was probably unpleasant."

Shit, she started crying and Masha joined her. I wasn't good at dealing with emotional women, and with nothing to say to comfort them, I gave them time to cry it out. Sara was a strong woman; finally she regained control of her emotions and started her story, first hesitantly and then with more confidence.

"You know that I taught history and Spanish literature at Kiev University in the seventies, but what you don't know is that I also taught Spanish at the KGB officers' school. I was rated as one of the best in Spanish and I was even offered a few times to move to Moscow headquarters to teach there."

With positive memories of Kiev uni, her voice strengthened.

"I liked Kiev, my academic achievements and prospects at the university looked good, that's why I didn't want to change anything. Besides, I never treated the language course with the KGB as my prime job. But then in 1978 or maybe beginning of 1979, my boss from the KGB courses called me to his office. Gennadiy Anatolyevich was a colonel, who I'd heard, spent a lot of time abroad and now was appointed to head the officers' courses as a sort of retirement from operational activity."

14

Sara smiled unintentionally. I took it that she might've liked this officer.

"Go on, please, Sara." I coaxed.

"So he asked me who was my best student, whose Spanish would pass for a native, even if it sounded like they were from another Spanish speaking country, and more importantly, who I thought was mature enough to act alone as a resident in a foreign country on an important liaison mission." She paused and sighed as the memories came flooding back.

"Please, go on." I prompted.

"Yes, I am sorry. We went over the list of the students, but rejected candidates one after another for different reasons. Naturally, it came to the point of whether I could do it myself. Gennadiy Anatolyevich explained passionately how this task was very important to the central committee of the Communist Party, that he had to send someone qualified, and besides, he argued, someone who really wants to master the language perfectly, cannot do it having never visited a place where this language is spoken and without interacting with real native speakers. He was very convincing. He promised that my academic research wouldn't be lost, and assured me that Kiev University would leave my position at the faculty unoccupied. I would have a very high salary, communist party diplomas would be awarded, and I would live comfortably like most distinguished comrades."

I smiled at Sara's words. Such hollow promises were extended daily by the Moscow elite. Sara saw my smile and paused.

"I know. Believing their lies makes me sound so naive. I was still a young girl, and not schooled in their ways."

15

"I understand," I answered truthfully. "We were all lied to and exploited by the Party."

Masha took her mother's hand in her own in a comforting gesture.

"It sounds silly now, but the colonel stressed how easy, yet very important the mission was. It sounded almost like the Party was sending me on a prestigious paid vacation combined with a Spanish practice course. Most of what he told was lies, as I discovered later. I don't know whether he himself knew that or believed in what he was saying. I was young and naive and I had no reason to doubt the words of my superior. In the end, he told me that if for some reason I had problems adapting, I should just advise my commander and, if I do it enough time in advance, let's say like three months, they would come up with a replacement, no problem."

Sara took a sip from a glass of water and I had a chance to consider what I just heard. Was I surrounded by spies from all directions? My best friend David turned out to be an Israeli Mossad collaborator. My mother-in-law was KGB in the past. Were I myself on some CIA mission in another dimension, while in a coma? CIA – because a former KGB chief wanted me dead, I started to wonder.

Sara resumed her story, so I had to concentrate.

"At that stage, I was already convinced I should go," she reasoned. "Now, I recalled that I hadn't asked which country we were talking about. During our conversation I imagined the royal palaces of Madrid, medieval architecture of Barcelona, or the ancient capital of Toledo. But Gennadiy said, 'Nicaragua.' Not something that I'd expected, and I struggled to remember anything about the country other than the occasional TASS announcements about the heroic struggle of the common people against the regime of the cruel capitalist dictator in that remote country. And that USSR couldn't stand aside, of course."

No doubt this was an unexpected and revealing story, but I started to fidget. Women never can get straight to the point and give just the punch line. All the time they beat about the bush. I inhaled deeply to calm myself down and relax a bit. Perhaps, if I led her slightly, it would help. Using a pause between the sentences I interrupted.

"So, a month or two later and you are in Nicaragua. What happened there?"

"Wait. It was more serious than that. I went through special training, learnt how to use a radio transmitter, memorised encryption cipher, excelled in ideology and so on, but I'll spare you the details."

She'd got the drift.

"I was travelling with a false Argentinean passport under the name of Maria Juanita De Oliveira. My orders were to get in touch with Pablo in Managua, who was supposed to put me in contact with the Sandinistas - the revolutionary partisans fighting the regime. I was to stay close and work with the local gang leader, sorry - revolutionist, known as *Garibaldi*. I was to provide him with radio contact with the Soviet intelligence office in Havana, coordinate supplies and ensure adherence to proletarian ideology. Managua, the capital, seemed nice, but the day after my arrival Pablo took me to the jungle to meet my new comrades, so I didn't have an opportunity to explore it properly. With all my belief in what I was doing, that their cause was just, and that it mirrored our ideology, I understood

17

within a week that it wasn't for me. Apart from the obvious inconvenience of living in the jungle, constantly on the move, those guys were barbarians. I just didn't fit in. On top of that I had a most acute allergy to some plant so most of the time I felt really asthmatic. They listened to my lectures, agreed with the ideology, claimed to strive for the equality and benefit of the people, but each night they hit the booze, cocaine, prostitutes and other vices. My Soviet colleagues didn't exactly oppose that, when along with the armament shipments were always cases of Stolichnaya."

Hmm, didn't sound that bad to me.

"Garibaldi and his subordinates paid me some respect in not trying anything funny, but I wasn't sure this attitude would last. So, on my first visit to our headquarters in Havana I submitted a request to resign and get back home. The Lieutenant there promised to pass it to his superiors and suggested they would consider it quickly. 'By the way, did you bring coke?' He asked me. I was shocked; I didn't know what to say. 'Next time you bring from Garibaldi a special package for our commanders here. They won't be pleased that you came empty-handed. Understood?' That was weird, but I still refused to believe they needed it for their own consumption. Nevertheless I left Havana heading back to the jungle with a hard feeling. I started to realise that I was in trouble. USSR was supporting the Sandinistas, USA the Contras and I was stuck in the middle, starting to have major doubts about my superiors."

"Did you meet the Puppet Master in Havana?" I helpfully suggested to keep Sara focused. I noticed that Masha was keeping silent during the entire conversation. That was untypical. She reclined on the sofa listening intently.

"No," Sara continued. "Two weeks after I left Havana I received a radiogram that I was to wait for someone in Managua at an undercover flat. I hoped that this someone was sent to replace me there, but couldn't believe it was happening so soon. That was Colonel Alexander Korablyov, chief of Soviet Intelligence headquarters in Havana, who came to meet me in the Managua outskirts. That's who they called the Puppet Master. He was the chief of the entire KGB operations in Latin America at that time."

She sobbed, hesitant again whether to continue. I patted her arm and moved a glass of water closer to her. Her expression hinted that we were approaching the most traumatic part.

"When I opened the door of the flat in a shabby residential building, someone was already there. A tall man with imperious countenance, dressed in civilian business-like clothes was standing in the living room. He said 'I'm Colonel Alexander Korablyov! Do you know who I am?' I greeted him saying that I did, as his name was always mentioned with reverence in Havana. I was really glad to see him; he was the first person from the motherland that I'd met in Nicaragua. 'Comrade Korablyov, it's nice to see a compatriot here.' I told him. 'Take your clothes off!' he ordered. 'What?' I thought I didn't hear it right, not being used to the Russian tongue during the last months. 'You heard me.' He looked angry. 'I don't like to repeat myself.' I wanted to ask why, when he grabbed me by my hair, turned me around and covered my mouth with his huge, sweaty palm. I tried to free myself, but his grip immediately turned tighter. I tried to kick him backwards with my legs. I don't know whether I missed or I hit him, it didn't make a difference. He was now holding my face with one hand from behind, then he just bent me over, tore my panties off and raped me. I was crying, yelling, trying to resist, but nothing helped. When he finished, he threw me to the corner of the room. I was completely exhausted, terrified, dejected and humiliated. He pulled out of his pocket a plastic bag, took some powder out of it, put it on the table, arranged a line and snorted it with a ten cordobas bill. Then he said something like: 'You bitch, hear me now. The Party sent you here because it's an important front of our global fight with the capitalist pigs. You stop thinking of yourself, *blyad*. If you are needed here, you stay put and perform the best you can. I don't accept any whining, complaints or resignations. By the way, if by any chance you would think of switching sides to the Contras or anything stupid, I can't guarantee a bright communist future to your parents in Kiev and your little brother Vasiliy.' I was in shock. How could he say such a thing?"

"That's awful," Masha whispered almost silently.

"I can't describe what I felt. He raped me two more times the same endless day. I don't know whether it was some cocaine side effect, but this man wasn't human. He was a cruel demon, the devil himself in human incarnation. I tried to stab him with a kitchen knife after he came out of the bathroom at some point, but he snatched it out of my hand and made a cut on my arm instead. He knocked me unconscious and when I woke up, he had already left."

Masha burst into tears and hugged her mother. They wept and they wept, while I sat and stared at the old scar on Sara's right arm and imagined the whole scene somewhere in

Nicaragua not that far away from the beautiful and peaceful Cayman Islands where we now sat. I was shocked. I had expected to hear a frustrated love story, some intimate character details that would help me understand my opponent. I didn't consider myself a sissy, but, boy, that was brutal. I embraced my wife and her mother, their eyes wet with tears, trying not to add my sobs to their crying chorus. After hearing all this, I was sure Masha wouldn't mind if I sent her father back to hell if such an opportunity arose.

Masha quieted and Sara was ready to finish her story.

"I won't describe to you further tortures that I suffered in that country. I didn't see him ever again. Soon enough, I discovered that I was pregnant, but that's when the uprising became especially violent and I didn't have an opportunity to reach any city. I was afraid of an abortion in the jungle, so, you Mashenka, were born in Nicaragua. I tried to hold on for you and myself and hoped to be able to run away some time."

Masha - born in Nicaragua? That's something I would've never imagined.

"So how did you manage to escape?" I asked.

"In 1979 the Sandinistas got the upper hand and Managua fell to their rule. Korablyov received a General's rank and was sent to a more burning part of the world - Afghanistan. I wasn't needed anymore, once the official USSR embassy was established, the new chief of the Havana office let me leave after first making sure that I wouldn't mouth off about what was going on there. I was ashamed and too broken to insist on an investigation and the KGB didn't want to put any blame on their prominent officer, whose star was on the rise, so as a compromise they conjured up a birth certificate for Masha, as if she was born in Kiev and let me retire quietly with my misery."

After this conversation, I went out to the veranda and looked casually at my son playing football with some local kids, with the goals set up between the coconut trees on my private beach. The perimeter was meticulously guarded by Arthur's teams with machine guns by their sides, ready for action. Arthur didn't even let them smoke together at the same time. Sunset was nearing and as the porch faced west, the ultimate view of the Caribbean sun taking a slow motion dive into the ocean was just fabulous. But this time my gaze wasn't fatherly or admiring. Considering that I wasn't the kindest type on the planet and discovering now what a monstrous grandfather my son had, I couldn't ignore my underlying concern. My son had got the deadliest set of genes, alright. Were we raising another Stalin or Hitler? Can education overcome pedigree? I hoped I lived long enough to find out.

Poor Sara. The roots of her usually dejected mood had been uncovered. No wonder she preferred to not say a word to her daughter all these years. I hoped my wife would be able to cope with this awful revelation.

***

I looked out of the airplane window. Nothing except for the Atlantic Ocean was visible in any direction, so we must've left the Caribbean behind already. I settled back in my seat and asked the crew to bring me something refreshing. Although I heard the story of Masha's conception only yesterday, I still hadn't quite got my head around the fact that she was the

Puppet Master's daughter. The only new facts about my opponent that I had derived were that he was a rapist, just as he was a killer, and that he probably was at some period a rather heavy cocaine consumer. If he continued with that hobby, in Afghanistan he must've switched to heroin and opium, because that's what you get in the Golden Crescent area, notoriously known to every drug trafficker. I knew that before too long I would be face to face with the monster who was actually my father-in-law. What an interesting meeting it was likely to be.

Glorious Kazakhstan

The plane entered a turbulent zone, which perfectly matched my inner anxiety. I saw the lightning forks all around and similarly I felt some almost electric discharges inside my soul. I couldn't hear the rattle of the thunder because of the humming of the turbines, instead I felt the pound of the fury inside my chest. But rage is a bad companion in these circumstances. Peter, my pilot, announced through the loudspeaker that he would try to switch to a different flight corridor to find a calmer route, but my mind was meandering far beyond the somewhat claustrophobic boundaries of the passenger compartment of the small private jet.

I expected the Puppet Master to pass on his regards once he discovered I was out of the coma, so I had intended on conjuring up a surprise of my own. Unfortunately he had beaten me to it, when he abducted Sasha. Surely, that was his way of saying hello. When I called Arthur straight after I'd learned of Sasha's kidnap, he had another piece of pertinent and shocking intel. The same day, Taras Balabolenko, the Defence Minister of Ukraine, had died suddenly and unexpectedly due to a heart attack, but Arthur's sources in the ministry revealed that signs of an injection were found on the minister's neck, right on the hairline. It was a well-known KGB trick, however any attempt to declare anything except for a natural death was quickly suppressed by the state prosecutor, eager to issue the coroner's report. Were Sasha's abduction and the Minister's demise, taking place almost simultaneously, just unrelated events? I doubted that very much. That was probably Taras' punishment for leaking the details of a conspiracy to my colleague, Boris.

Arthur had rightly shut me down when I suggested we meet up in Moscow, but I hadn't thrown the plan out completely. If my own plan failed, then Moscow would be the only option I had left. Before it came to that, I had one other throw of the dice. My choice of destination was hopefully not on the Puppet Master's radar - Astana, the capital of Kazakhstan.

My partner in an aluminium business, and no less importantly, my good friend, Oleg headed one of the five clans that controlled the Kazakh economy under the auspices of the Aqsaqal, as they called their president. I thought that if Aqsaqal would ask his Moscow peer to send over the Puppet Master right away to discuss some serious security issues, the latter would facilitate the Puppet Master's arrival, at least out of curiosity and as a courtesy to the very close relations between the countries. If the Puppet Master didn't go, or it wasn't him who held Sasha, or if I was unable to resolve the issue if he did turn up, then the Moscow plan would be my final play.

I didn't know exactly how well Oleg was connected to the president. He claimed he was very close, even friendly, but all of us tend to exaggerate such things. Now, I was to find out the true value of his words. After hearing my initial request and not turning it down, even sparing me the necessity to explain the background, he returned my call almost instantaneously, claiming that my plan was doable and Aqsaqal had agreed to help, provided that I comply with whatever terms his brokerage would require, and whatever the outcome of the arrangement, it would not ruin his relations with Moscow.

So far so good. I was a little worried about agreeing to something up front without knowing what it involved, but with limited choices, I had to play the hand I had been dealt.

The courtesy, especially in central Asia was that I needed to show and verify my deepest respect and choose a present that would relay those feelings. Only now did that fact come to my mind. Of course, I had forgotten to arrange anything with all the urgency and fuss. Why the fuck did I retain five secretaries and assistants, if no one reminded me of this shit when I really needed them to? I was really upset at my oversight, but I could blame no-one but myself, seeing as I hadn't told anyone where I was going and who I was going to meet.

I checked my watch and calculated the time difference with Kazakhstan. Hmm, it was getting late there, and borderline for calling someone at such an hour. Nevertheless, I needed to sort the problem out, so I picked up the satellite phone that I used during flights and dialled Oleg again.

"Hey, Oleg, it's me again. I'm on the way. Just passing through some fucking Atlantic storm, so I hope you can still hear me. Do you?"

"Yeah, Misha, I do. Open the window for a sec, let me hear the thunder, ha-ha-ha!"

Oleg was enjoying himself, probably picturing me struggling with the emergency exit.

"What time are you arriving?"

He sounded bright and alert, so I was glad my call hadn't woken him.

"You'll see me first thing in the morning, bro. I'm supposed to land just after 8 am, if we refuel quickly enough in Lisbon. I'm sure you don't wake up earlier than that. You know, I had to plan the route so as not to enter Russian airspace? I can't be too careful these days, my friend," I complained.

"Misha, you scare me. It's probably dangerous to be associated with you. I'll re-think whether I want to come meet you at the airport tomorrow or maybe it'll be wiser to erase your number from my cell phone?" Oleg laughed again.

"To tell you the truth, you *should be* concerned. I can boast one attempted assassination, another one intercepted and one blown-up building in little more than a month. Maybe even now some Russian sputnik is taking aim at my plane."

I picked up Oleg's joking manner and played along.

"Listen, Oleg, I need some advice from you. What should I bring for Aqsaqal? What do you think would impress him?"

"That's easy, Misha, but I'm not sure you have time to arrange it."

"What is it?"

"Bring him a horse."

It was my turn to burst out laughing.

"Oleg, man, be serious for a second. It's as you said, I don't have much time to arrange something decent."

"I am serious, Misha. That's what he likes, that's his passion. He collects them and has quite a large collection of fine horses. If you bring him some rare pure-breed, I guarantee he'll be impressed. Do you have enough room on your Gulfstream jet?

Because, if so, you might stop over in Andalusia to pick up a decent stud."

I still couldn't stop laughing at this bizarre idea. I knew that many rulers and nouveau riches collected horses, but until now I hadn't encountered any.

"Oleg, I have a better idea. I can bring over an American banker who snorts like a horse. And if he hears some shots in the air, he might outrun Aqsaqal's best racers!"

I was still trying to control the chuckling.

"Ha-ha-ha, up to you, Misha. I trust in your taste for originality. Have a safe flight, I'll see you tomorrow."

"Thank you, Oleg. See you soon."

Well, at least Oleg managed to alleviate my sour and angry mood. Now I needed to find a purebred stud and get it to Kazakhstan in just a few hours.

Why didn't this guy collect rabbits or donkeys, at least, so I could take them aboard? I dialled Johnny - the American banker who worked for me. No, I didn't really plan to present him as a horse, but I was already anticipating how I would josh him with this bizarre idea. His phone rang and rang and rang and he didn't answer. That was strange. I hoped he hadn't been kidnapped too, because I wouldn't pay a ransom for him. Who else did I have for this task?

I called David, my best friend ever since our student years and one of my closest business associates. He was more apt for this mission anyway. Although he was my friend, I didn't have time for small talk. After waiting for several rings, I heard something that vaguely resembled a masculine voice. At least he answered.

"Listen, Dave, I need your help right now. Please, put aside anything you've been doing and do as follows. Do you have anyone serious in Spain?"

I heard something vaguely affirmative. Did I interrupt him shagging or what? I was sure I heard some giggles on the other end, muffled by his hand over the mouthpiece.

"You do? Good. I hope it's not someone from Spanish intelligence, because I'm pretty sick of spies lately. No? Good. I need you to arrange for someone to buy a horse."

Again, David mumbled in reply.

"Not a *whore*, blyad suka! Your perverted mind cannot grasp anything else. A *h-o-r-s-e*," I spelled it for him. "No time for questions. It has to be a real beauty with impeccable pedigree and whatever else is necessary, with all the papers or manuals, I don't understand shit about this. But you make sure it's a real diamond, something that I wouldn't be ashamed to give to the Sheikh of Kuwait."

"Kuwait?"

"No, no, I'm not going to Kuwait. Just figuratively speaking. Now, you or whoever you put on this task has to charter a transport aircraft, like, a Boeing. Load the horse and a shepherd, or whatever they are called - a cowboy? And send the plane to Astana. The horse, the plane and the shepherd must be there by 0800 hours Kazakh time tomorrow."

David started to barrage me with questions. Fair enough, but I had no time to go through the plan with him.

"Listen Dave, just do it. I'll call you later to give you details. I can't explain everything now. Thanks, bro, I appreciate your help. Use any resources you need - my Kiev office, Tel Aviv staff, whatever. This is paramount. Tell whoever you need it's

29

my direct order. I count on you, man. Please, get to it; you don't have time for another blowjob, please."

I was sure it would be sorted. The whole operation would cost me a fortune: horse, charter, cowboy and the inevitable bribes, but I would make a good impression both on Aqsaqal and on Oleg. I didn't usually grant blank cheques to anyone, but this was for the sake of my brother. I hoped my money would be spent well this time. What did I need it for, if not to save my blood?

These preparations were just a prelude. I was busying myself with auxiliary stuff, so as not to tackle the prime issue, of which I was subconsciously afraid. When it came down to basics, what would I do if the Puppet Master arrived in Astana? How would I convince him to release my brother and take the hit order off me? Good fucking questions, which I didn't yet have an answer to. I needed to prepare such arguments that no trump could beat.

***

I didn't get any sleep on the jet, as my mind wouldn't let me rest. When you travel against the clock, descending in time zones, you can't tell if it is a night or a day that you miss. I calculated that I had been awake for over twenty four hours. No problem, I thought, whilst in a coma I'd accumulated enough sleep reserves to see me through the next day.

Maybe it's because I have a shitty character, but I couldn't just let others carry out their tasks without my close supervision. I handled the entire operation hands on, calling David and others that were involved in getting the horse,

Masha to see that everything was okay with her, Sara and the children, and Arthur, just to get him upset that I was compromising our preparations by going online.

"Dave, by the way, once you make sure the horse is on the way, please, contact Johnny and tell him that I'm looking for him." I ordered David during our umpteenth conversation. "When's the last time you saw or spoke with him?"

"Now that you are asking, I haven't seen him for quite a while," David replied. "He was in Israel at our top management meeting that we arranged a few days after you were shot, but I don't think I've seen him after that. Definitely not after you woke up."

Something wasn't right. Johnny wouldn't forget to check in, and with his responsibilities, he was supposed to be at my beck and call 24/7.

"Something is wrong, David. I have a bad feeling, and from your tone, I think you do too. Take care of Johnny after you finish with the horse. The horse is more important than the banker at the moment."

I hung up and called Vera, my in-flight assistant, to fetch me a double espresso and an energy drink. She had been warming up the lunch, and the smell of chicken Kiev was already wafting through the plane. Beside the drinks, it was nice watching her wriggling up the aisle in her sexy stewardess mini-skirt, and even nicer when she turned and bent to get something from the mini fridge just to the side of my in-flight office.

"Yes, I am definitely still alert," I said to myself with a wry smile, as a glimpse of suspenders and bare thighs just above, pushed all thoughts of horses and missing bankers momentarily from my brain.

"Thanks, Vera. I'll need many of these to stay awake. Oh, and can you please check our parachutes? I've just received information that a Russian Sukhoy squadron scrambled from Ryazan military airport to intercept our plane."

Seeing the startled expression on Vera's perfectly made up face, I quickly reassured her.

"I'm joking, girl. Relax, go have some rest. If I need more coffee, I'll take it myself".

I must have been more tired than I realised, I thought. That wasn't such a funny joke.

Oleg called again with the good news that the Puppet Master was on his way to Astana, supposedly arriving just half an hour or so after me. I asked Oleg to arrange the most lengthy protocol ceremony for his arrival, to give us - me, Oleg and the president - more time to prepare.

In between all the telephone calls, I was contemplating the situation, trying to predict how the upcoming meeting would go. What did I know? The Puppet Master had some kind of plan for the restoration of the USSR, starting with Ukraine, and I was an obstacle to it, or so it appeared. Yes, I could pull some strings in Ukraine, but I couldn't claim to be overly influential on its current regime. So, truthfully, I didn't know what this guy's motivation in wanting me out of the way was.

Now, what could I possibly offer him? Money? I didn't think that interested him. Drugs? I was quite sure his secret agencies ran much more successful drug trafficking businesses than my own humble connections. Maybe I could offer him free entrance to home games at Watford United, my English football club? I was thinking and brainstorming and coffee-drinking, but no matter what I did, I still didn't have any leverage on my nemesis. But he had plenty on me, by holding my brother captive. Shit, shit, shit.

In these circumstances I came to the conclusion that I had to rely heavily on the Kazakh Aqsaqal. He was someone in the same league as my opponents and if he were to intervene on my behalf, I was sure the Puppet Master would respect his request. I, for my part, could only promise to be out of the way for whatever plans this Korablyov had. Not much, but if I was out, I hoped there would be no reason to slaughter me and my brother. That is, of course, unless there was more to my predicament than I was aware of. This wasn't my war anyway, it concerned states, not individuals, so why should I endanger myself and those close to me for Ukraine's cause? It had an army, albeit heavily depleted by lack of funding, ineptitude, theft and legal and illegal sales abroad, security services, although they were probably infiltrated by the Russians, and a 'democratic' government which seemed to be more money motivated than patriotic. Definitely, I was out!

Can I call that a plan? Of course, not. But my deliberations looked sound to me. Since Aqsaqal had agreed to see me and invited the Puppet Master, I assumed he was already willing to help to some degree. Now I just needed to convince him to intervene on my behalf.

Upon landing the spring started to uncoil very fast. Oleg picked me up at the airfield, and we immediately set off for the Presidential Palace. I was really glad to see him. His cruel, but at the same time playful smile hadn't changed since the last time I saw him in London, half a year ago. I could understand why people feared him when his grey eyes were focused on them as if ready to fire a laser beam, but for me he was a true friend who I trusted completely.

It was funny that when we first met in the reception chamber of a Tajik official, we almost strangled each other, were it not for Arthur separating us. We were both going for the same concession in Tajikistan and had the same level of connections. Then, the Chairman of Natural Resources Committee invited us to his office, while we were still planning how to get rid of each other after the audience. However, after a couple of rounds of vodka, we felt some rare instinctive connection and like-mindedness in each other. By the end of the meeting with the Chairman, and after weighing up the pros and cons of the deal, we decided to go for the tender together.

Only later did I learn that Oleg's nickname in the underworld was Zeus, the father of the gods, for he managed to ruthlessly subdue all the local drug lords and barons of greater Almaty for the first time in over seventy years. He was a real criminal authority with distinctive rules he followed doggedly, with a natural dignity unlike the pretenders who indulged in *bespredel* - ignorant of any rules or gangster code.

My jet landed at Astana International Airport just before 8am and was instructed to taxi to the furthermost corner of the airport, well away from prying eyes. No formalities were needed as Oleg waited to greet me when I exited the plane, and ushered me into a black limousine bearing just some symbols instead of letters and numbers on the number plate.

Oleg looked healthy and refreshed, spreading throughout the car the rich odour of expensive au de cologne, the polar opposite to my own appearance and smell. He was dressed formally, which was a contrast with his usual impudent, somewhat vulgar behaviour. He was not akin to the Kazakh people and his smartly trimmed blonde-grey bristles and Caucasian facial features pointed towards European ancestry. But he had been born in Almaty and lived his entire life there, just like many other originally Slavic families.

"Misha, my friend, it is good to see you," he said with his usual wicked smile. "I assume the Russians didn't hear about your little vacation here, no? I didn't hear on the news about any mysterious plane crashes last night, so I thought I'd better come and meet you."

"Thanks Oleg, nothing would surprise me these days, so I am just happy to have my feet on solid ground. Tell me, did my gift arrive safely?"

"Yes, my friend. I don't know how you managed it in such a short time, but you have bought quite an impressive beast. I'm not too proficient, but I've learnt a thing or two about them. Your stud will fit proudly into Aqsaqal's collection."

"Well, I'm glad you liked it. No secret here, I just didn't put a cap on its purchase price, insisting it must be worthy of an emperor. Are we going to the Presidential Palace?" I asked, nervous about the tight schedule and in a hurry to leave the airport to avoid accidentally running into the Puppet Master before I was ready. I knew I had an advantage on him, but instinctively I was wary.

"In a short while. I didn't feel comfortable to ask for a meeting before 9 am," Oleg replied. He seemed relaxed. That was good, helping to ease my anxiety.

"Now I know the method of how to bring you over, my friend. My invitation to come visit me in Kazakhstan was never enough, huh? I need to abduct someone dear to make you

35

move. At least that brings you here. We'll have breakfast with Aqsaqal, I'm quite sure, so let me show you around before we head to the palace."

I knew that central Asia, rich in raw materials, offered unique business opportunities, but except for Tajikistan I hadn't travelled to those backwater places before.

"How about we see Borat's monument on the way, Oleg, I want to see this fabulous Kazakh." I teased.

"Hey, Misha you don't mention him here. Not even joking. I hope Aqsaqal won't make the connection that you are Jewish and the guy playing him was too. That pornography of a film is an insult to this proud country. The peasants weren't even Kazakh, they were just some fuckers."

"Maybe, but it's fucking funny!" I couldn't help teasing my old friend.

Oleg looked at my stern face as I struggled to prevent a smile spreading across my lips.

"You fucker," he finally said when I could control myself no longer. "Okay...maybe it contains a few funny parts, and maybe a few truths we don't like to admit. But don't ever mention that to Aqsaqal!"

We entered some futuristic district and I turned my head in all directions to take in the scenery. It was clear that there was a proud leader in power, as the city looked tidy, modern and heavily invested in. We passed near a huge tower with an enormous ball or globe on its top.

"That's Baiterek," Oleg explained, "It symbolises the moving of the capital to Astana from Almaty. Nice, huh? Our boss invests in bringing in prominent world architects for these things. There are some very impressive projects around," Oleg said proudly. "And there you see, behind it, the building with a spear? That's Akorda - where we are going."

A few gigantic buildings came into view, all somehow connected architecturally, forming the axis of the city master plan.

"Astana was planned and built from scratch," Oleg continued. "The advantages of moving the capital here were numerous - not least because of the Kazakh majority here rather than the Slavs."

I sensed some distaste in Oleg's statement, but chose not to push him.

"Investment has increased many times over, we have a new airport, decent infrastructure, and in a few years an extensive rapid transit system. We now have students from all over the world coming to our prestigious universities."

The pride in Oleg's voice was highly evident, and not unwarranted. I had expected horse carts and hovels, but Astana was modern, clean and had some spectacular architecture.

The last building resembled the Kiev Parliament edifice. The top, formed by the glass dome and a spear were very similar as well as the colonnade at the entrance. I bet it had an excellent view of the Ishim River from its rear windows.

Now my heart started to pump rapidly in my chest again. I didn't feel ready, and the crucial moments were closing in. My palms were sweaty and my hands trembled a little. I'd just drank too many cups of coffee on the plane, I hoped.

We approached the gate of the presidential compound, the car slowed, and an officer, recognising the car as it neared, hurried to open the gate in advance, saluting us as we passed by and proceeded towards the parking area.

A beautiful young oriental woman wearing a beige formal suit coat with matching skirt, a broad and open smile on her face, was waiting for us as we exited the car. The smile was natural and welcoming, not artificially strained. Unfortunately it was not for me, but for Oleg, who returned the smile and gestured towards me. The woman nodded in my direction, and spoke.

"Good morning, Mr Vorotavich. I hear that you've flown here from the other side of the globe. Come, let me offer you something inside before you have your audience."

"Thank you, that would be most welcome," I replied.

"Hi Damira," Oleg said to the woman, "you look especially beautiful this morning. How's the Boss? In good spirits?"

Damira blushed slightly, and before she could respond, Oleg turned to me and said: "This is our Boss' favourite assistant, Misha. Ms Damira is a very influential woman in this country. Through her influence on President Zhanbolat Tirsynbekov, she administers the state affairs more than any minister in this city."

"Oh, Mr Oleg, you definitely exaggerate my role in this country. I'm just a junior state official, Mr Vorotavich, nothing more. Don't pay attention to your friend's flattery. As for your question, Oleg, we haven't yet seen the Boss this morning, but he'll be around any moment."

At the security post, Oleg asked me to leave my mobile phone with the guards and led me through the metal detector. Damira took charge from there and led us while we followed behind along a broad and well illuminated corridor. Although preoccupied with the upcoming encounter I couldn't help noticing Damira's rocking ass right in front of us. I assumed an appreciative look, and shifted my gaze to Oleg to ask the unspoken "question" understandable to every man. Oleg smiled, grasping immediately that I was curious whether or not he had fucked her. He shook his head and shot his eyes upwards. I derived from that that maybe the president did.

Not bad, not bad. I shook the distraction from my mind.

We reached the elevators and I was very impressed by the rich and thoughtful decoration and interior design of the building. Every detail seemed to have some meaning - some taken from local Asian folklore and others reflecting a European heritage. The decor was opulent without being garish or over the top, and hinted that world class designers had been involved with the recent palace refurbishment.

We disembarked on the third floor and Damira ushered us into the Oval hall and through to the far end, where another door led to a smaller room, where the table was already set for refreshments. The room was windowless, so I assumed it was internal and probably designed to host more intimate conversations, reducing the chance of remote eavesdropping from the outside. The white ceiling had spot-lighting around it, directed upwards to give the feeling of natural light. The thick carpets swallowed any sounds, so the waiters approaching from behind us moved silently to the table without attracting my attention until they were stood in front of us.

As before, the decor was tasteful, and luxury was hinted at, rather than thrown in the visitor's face. I didn't see dozens of portraits and statues of President Tirsynbekov at every turn unlike the premises of many other dictators from this part of the world who mostly seemed to suffer from a Napoleonic complex.

The massive throne-like chair at the head of a table didn't leave any doubts as to where the host would sit, so Oleg and I occupied the chairs on the left and right side from it, so that we were sitting opposite each other.

Damira poured us a refreshing drink that was a mixture of freshly-squeezed fruits and then she left the room. There was another door at the end of the room, where two soldiers, wearing ceremonial uniform were standing, each holding a Kalashnikov assault rifle with a shining blade attached underneath its barrel.

After a few minutes, the guarded door opened and a tall man entered. The soldiers immediately stood to attention and saluted him in perfect harmony. Oleg and I scrambled to our feet and walked towards him. A tall, slightly overweight man, he wore a military uniform, heavily decorated with insignia and ribbons. I suspected that Oleg had told him that the meeting had some militaristic inclination, more so since a former Soviet KGB chief was invited along too.

On first inspection, I estimated he was around fifty years of age. I cursed myself for not spending some time on the internet studying some background on my host. That would have been the wisest thing to do, and it irritated me that I had overlooked it. Despite my anger at myself, I smiled broadly, as Oleg introduced me to the President of Kazakhstan.

"Your Excellency, may I introduce Mikhail Leonidovich Vorotavich - a prominent business shark, philanthropist, philosopher and footballer, no - football producer."

Yeah, I got it. Oleg *was* in friendly relations with the president, if he could say such bollocks to him.

The president smiled, dismissed the intro by telling Oleg to stop clowning around and gestured to us both to return to our seats. He occupied his chair and offered that we fill our plates with the snacks on offer. It wasn't a continental breakfast for sure, as I eyed an assortment of meats, cheeses, salads, baked fish and other stuff that looked unfamiliar. I kept silent, expecting Oleg to start and then let me present my business.

"Please, Mr Vorotavich, you must try the kazy, it is excellent at the moment," the president said, gesturing to a plate laden with what closely resembled sausages.

"And try the manti," Oleg said, pointing at a bowl filled with little parcels that looked like dim sum. "You must dip them in the sour cream, they are delicious!"

I played the perfect guest, and tucked into the local dishes. They were surprisingly delicious, but I wasn't there to sample the cuisine - I was desperate to get down to business as I knew the Puppet Master had probably landed already, and would be en route to the palace as we ate. I caught Oleg's gaze and hoped he understood my desperation to start the conversation. The president beat him to it.

"Mr Vorotavich, you've come all the way down here, and I agreed to accept you for an urgent reason, as our mutual friend Oleg here has updated me in general terms in regards to your present predicament. Furthermore, on Oleg's request, I have invited retired General Korablyov, who is nonetheless the advisor to my Russian colleague on security issues and, diplomatically speaking, he is a very forceful and powerful man. By the way, I have been informed that a Russian military plane with him on board is on approach. I wouldn't be doing all this were it not for a few good reasons, which are in descending order: Kazakh national security, my friend's request and my natural inclination to help people. Having said that, I'm not entirely convinced, whether and to what degree if at all, I want to intervene. Perhaps, hearing you out will help me to decide."

I was still holding my fork with a piece of salmon on it, as it seemed rude to eat while he was addressing me. I had a whirl of simultaneous thoughts and impressions. Wow, this man was sharp and to the point. Impressive. I didn't know that the Puppet Master was moved around by the Russian Air Force. Shit, that meant that he had the official backing of the establishment. But I didn't have time to digest this information further as two pairs of eyes were on me, waiting for my reply.

The life of my brother as well as my own, and maybe even my family, depended on whether I managed to convince Aqsaqal that it was in his best interests to help me out. I felt a cold sweat forming in my armpits, but I tried to assume a relaxed and confident persona. Measuring carefully what I was saying, I stated my case in a steady and unhurried voice.

"Mr President, thank you very much for finding the time to see me and to dedicate some thought to my situation. Even if you decide not to intervene, you have my sincere gratitude, and I'm in debt to you for this."

I put the fork down, arranging my thoughts into order and hesitating whether to mention the horse.

"The reason that I told Oleg that it's not just my private situation, but it has a broader international meaning was because of a very dangerous conspiracy that came to my knowledge almost accidentally, a situation that could have a global significance."

I paused for a second and wiped my mouth. I needed to be careful not to exaggerate and remain credible.

"I must be frank, revealing to you the pieces of information that I have, is not entirely altruistic on my part, as I need your help to free my brother. Nonetheless, I hope that what I say will be useful to you and allow you to prepare for upcoming events."

I took a sip from whatever Damira poured us and resumed my little speech.

"Now, I will get straight to the point. I have serious grounds to believe that a cross-nations high-level conspiracy is being cooked, aimed at the restoration of the former Soviet Union, probably under a new brand name. At first, it's designed to reunite Russia, Ukraine and Belarus. Again, being honest, I cannot tell whether Kazakhstan is on the agenda at any stage, but as you well know the appetite comes with the food, so if the initial part is a success, then further steps may follow."

I noticed how the president moved uneasily in his chair. For sure, this was the worst nightmare of any leader of a former soviet republic. Oleg's arrogant, self-confident expression changed into a frown. I had definitely caught their attention. Now I had to capitalise on it.

"Except for two people: the notorious Puppet Master, who's involved, if not the main plotter, and the Ukrainian minister of defence, may he rest in peace, I don't know who else is implicated, but judging from these two, I can safely assume that several high level military and security figures are in the mix. The level of the two known participants may hint at how high this conspiracy goes. One doesn't have to be a genius to trace the chain of events that whenever some former republic strives to leave Russian orbit, it begins to experience all sorts of troubles and sometimes direct assault. Let's consider a few examples: Pridnestrovie region - the unrecognised republic is a former or current part of Moldova, severed from it with the backing of a third party army. Abkhazia is, or was a part of Georgia. Same scenario. Any internal separatism is also brutally suppressed, reflecting the Russian tendency. And who's the bully or the patron? Your biggest and closest neighbour. But now, it seems to me they don't want to be reactive any more, but change the mode to proactive. Some hot heads in Moscow or Saint Petersburg start to re-evaluate the dissolution process of 1991, feeling not too happy with the draw and want to reverse it. I've had some meetings in the States recently and those who are competent, corroborate my theory along with my own analytic team, which I've handpicked from the most prominent former intelligence communities. As Ukraine is drifting towards joining the European Union, I think we are on the verge of something big and potentially catastrophic."

I felt I'd driven my message right home. After a few moments, Oleg spoke to fill the uncomfortable silence, and probably to let Aqsaqal consider my information a little longer.

"Wow, Misha, with all this knowledge, assumptions, theories, connections in the States, analytic teams and think tanks, it is no wonder you attract assassination attempts every week or so. That's some unbelievable, surrealistic picture that you depict here."

"Thanks for the comforting words, Oleg. This week, nobody tried to slay me yet. I hope the soldiers that you have here would protect me, if the Puppet Master jumps on me when we meet."

I had no choice, but to play along with this black humour on my own account. Now the president joined the conversation.

"That's some interesting story you are trying to sell us here. I might have my own indications, confirming some of your assumptions, I'll check with my people later. Thank you for this insight about our neighbour's plan, if such a thing indeed exists. Even if some of it is incorrect, it's never unwise to check our preparedness to any eventuality. Now, how do you think I can help you with *your* situation?"

That's exactly the question that I was waiting for, and had rehearsed many different answers to it in my mind.

"Mr President, I would appreciate very much, if you would condescend to call me your personal friend in front of Korablyov and ask him to facilitate the release of my brother Alexander, held hostage in Moscow, as a personal favour to you. Of course, this guy would never admit that it's him holding my brother, but if he says he'll look into it, I'm sure my brother will be released very soon. I know it's insolent of me, but I've grave suspicions that unless it's your direct and unequivocal request, my brother won't make it beyond a couple of days maximum."

Aqsaqal eyed me closely as he considered my words. I needed to offer something, so I continued.

"In return, I'll be the most fervent Kazakh friend in Ukraine and I will do my best to promote whatever Kazakh people may have an interest in there. Also, I don't know on which Puppet Master's toes I've unintentionally stepped on, but I can promise to reverse any activity that might be seen as hostile to him, as long as I'm not personally affected by any of his plans."

Oleg joined in rhetorically: "Misha's word is his bond, Your Excellency. I have known him for many years, and if he says he will do something, one can be sure it will be done."

A secretary or an assistant entered for a second, bowed, put a small notice in front of the president and left the room. I darted a thankful gaze in Oleg's direction in the meantime, grateful that he had backed me up and been reverential in his address to his president. He noticed, and nodded subtly. The president read the note and turned to me.

"I'll try to facilitate your request, Mikhail. I don't know whether it's within my powers, but I will ask our Russian friend to help with the release of your brother. You make a good impression on me and you have a very good reference from Oleg. I trust normal relations far more than solemn obligations. It's not a condition to anything, but I know you are a parliament member in Ukraine and I'd appreciate if you join the Ukrainian-Kazakh inter-parliamentary friendship panel. I need positively oriented lawmakers there."

"Treat it as done, Your Excellency." I interrupted enthusiastically. I stood up and shook Aqsaqal's hand, thanking him like a little boy. "I really, really appreciate your willingness to help."

He dismissed my gratitude, as if it was nothing.

"Also, may it not sound liberal, but I don't let any foreigners do business in our country, unless they have good credentials. I want Oleg here to show you some of my state programs, ones that may benefit from external investment and expertise. I'm sure you will find some of them interesting and potentially profitable."

I nodded in agreement.

"And lastly, I want to thank you for your kind contribution of quite an interesting stallion, to our modest stud farm, and I'm looking forward to taking a proper look at him after these meetings."

I smiled and nodded, congratulating myself because I hadn't mentioned the stallion myself. This was a sincere accolade and not something induced by me.

"I was advised that our mutual friend is here, so I'll join him in the main hall. Stay here and I'll send someone to call you in soon."

Aqsaqal wiped his mouth with a napkin, stood and nodded, and walked towards the door from which we had entered.

I released a sigh of relief and leaned across the table and offered Oleg my hand.

"I owe you one, man."

The first part was over. I started to drum my fingers in nervous anticipation of meeting the man who according to all my information desperately wanted me dead.

***

I didn't feel like eating while we waited to be called in to the main hall, even though there were many dishes I hadn't tried that looked very appetising. I knew I shouldn't have, but I poured myself a large cup of black coffee, feeling that my nervousness had climbed another level.

"Oleg, by the way, I suggest you stay here in this room and don't come out to meet the Puppet Master. Joking aside, it's truly not recommended to be my friend these days, especially in front of this guy."

I knew Oleg would spurn my request, but I still felt like I needed to warn him.

"Misha, really, stop trying to frighten me, my friend. I'm shaking already, if that's what you want to know. I'm not afraid of anyone, especially in my own home, but these Russian bastards are very different to the usual scum I have to deal with. You've asked for my help and I'm here for whatever it takes. This is what friendship is about, however clichéd it may sound."

I nodded in appreciation of Oleg's words. After half an hour, the same girl that brought a note to the president, entered the room and suggested that we join the meeting in the Oval Hall. I let Oleg go first, staying a little behind his back. I wanted to appear in front of the Puppet Master unexpectedly and catch a glimpse at his reaction when he realised who was joining the meeting. My intuition told me that the president might not have revealed yet that I was going to be present.

The table in the huge Oval Hall was much bigger and as before, the president was sat at its head, while his guests were to his right hand side. As I appeared from behind Oleg's back, someone who wasn't watching closely wouldn't have noticed any change in the Puppet Master's posture or demeanour, but I *was* watching, and I swear I saw a spark of hatred in his eyes and an almost imperceptible instinctive twitch of his right arm in the direction of where the gun would be if he hadn't have given it over to the Kazakh security guys on arrival at the Presidential Palace.

'So, you are surprised, motherfucker,' I thought to myself, pleased that I'd made the old bastard uncomfortable.

Oleg and I went straight to the opposite side of the table to avoid any hint of a handshake. It was good that the president didn't insist on that, because I would've pounded the fucker rather than shaken his hand.

The Puppet Master was in the company of some Kazakh general, who looked much older than Korablyov. They were probably the same age, but Korablyov still exuded power even in the way he was sitting. Sara's description of him was still accurate, even though it referred to someone who was thirty five years younger. The icy unwavering stare of his light grey eyes, I was certain, hadn't changed at all from his younger years - they betrayed the cold blooded killer inside.

Suddenly all the rage, hatred and despair that I'd accumulated over the past few months could be attached to a physical object. I knew that whatever we agreed and decided here or elsewhere, this world was too small to bear both of us. That sounds like a cliché but that's exactly what I felt. His eyes never left mine as I took my seat, and I'm sure he knew exactly what I was thinking. A hint of a smile played on his lips. He had read my thoughts, and he was pleased. I immediately regretted that I'd abandoned my plan B, which was to intercept and *greet* the Puppet Master's car with few RPG's in Astana on the way from the airport to the president's residence.

In contrast to our silent exchange of lethal curses, the atmosphere around the table was extremely cordial with barely a hint of artificiality.

"Alexander," the president addressed the Puppet Master like an old friend. "I want to introduce to you these two gentlemen. This bald man is Oleg Talalayev," Aqsaqal said, gesturing to Oleg, who nodded in response. "He's a prominent local businessman and good friend to me and the Kazakh people."

Aqsaqal's gaze then moved along to me.

"And this is Mikhail Vorotavich. You probably don't know him, he's from Ukraine, and he's a very close friend of mine."

It was a world class performance. I knew from Oleg that the president hated this Puppet Master ever since he eavesdropped on a scornful remark at some Moscow gathering. The Puppet Master had been holding court with a group of lower ranked officers, and had remarked that except for the legendary Kim, he had never encountered a prominent Asian leader, and all the pathetic chieftains of -stan countries were just small fish. Aqsaqal took it as a personal insult and had never forgotten. However from the way Aqsaqal was speaking with the Puppet Master, an outsider would think they were best friends catching up on old times and planning a fishing trip for the weekend. I was such a rookie in political role playing in comparison with these two!

"Oh, Mr President, what a surprise," the Puppet Master replied with just the right amount of respect that he wanted - which was not too much. "You know that I'm informed on certain issues, but I never before heard you had close friends in Ukraine. It must be something fresh."

Although he was a guest with inferior formal status, it somehow felt that he was the boss in this meeting and not the president. Having been impressed with Aqsaqal's sharp instincts already, I was sure the president noticed it too and wouldn't have liked it. No such feelings were projected when

Aqsaqal spoke again, without bothering to answer the Puppet Master's comment.

"It's of course, not such a big issue, compared to what we were discussing before."

It became immediately clear to everyone in the room that what he was going to raise now was the main reason for holding this meeting.

"Mikhail has a little trouble in Moscow and I thought it would be a perfect opportunity to utilise your visit here to sort it out. His brother, Sasha Vorotavich, was abducted and is being held in Moscow. I know that you, Alexander, don't stand for such things and if anyone can help my friend, it's definitely you with your total control on the White Stone City."

Puppet Master nodded, and steepled his fingers in a grand gesture of considering the request.

"If that's your request, Mr President, you know that we never turn our closest friends down. Can you give me some details, please?"

The Puppet Master now turned to me, as it was a logical question to ask. We held each other's gaze and I could almost feel the force of venom and hatred directed towards me.

I gave a short account of the circumstances, including the exact time of the phone call I received in the Cayman Islands, my number there, along with the number displayed on my screen, the demands and my brother's description. I tried to act calm, cool and without emotion. It was all just a game; no doubt this guy knew perfectly well what had happened and every detail of both the kidnapping and Sasha's present whereabouts.

The Puppet Master took his phone out, dialled someone and in metallic, commanding tones dictated the details that I had just given and added, "find and release him, and punish whoever did it."

Then he turned to us and smiled.

"I hope my assistants can help, Mr President and Mr Vorotavich."

The president assumed a very pleased expression.

"I knew you were the person who could help in these tragic circumstances. The brother of my friend is also my friend. I believe now, Misha, that with Mr Korablyov's kind involvement you need not fear for your brother's destiny anymore. Right?"

He turned again to the Puppet Master, who nodded coldly but affirmatively.

"By the way, Mikhail here says that he might not be that likable in the eyes of the Russian establishment. Do you know by any chance what could be the reason for this enmity?"

A look of surprise flashed across the Puppet Master's face. It was a micro-expression that was quickly tamed as he returned to his usual stony expression.

"Well, as you mention it, I recall that Mr Vorotavich was the first Ukrainian with political and business leverage to start preaching for Ukraine's European integration. Many in Russia consider this direction as anti-Russian."

His voice rose as he said the final two words, unable to hide the menace behind them. He smiled slightly, a cold smile that never made its way to his eyes, and went back to the metallic monotone he had used when speaking on the telephone.

"That may well be a reason for any hostility that Mr Vorotavich feels is directed at him."

"Oh, if that's the reason," Aqsaqal said, "I had a small conversation with my friend just recently and he assured me that hurting Russian interests is the last thing that he desires. I'm confident that from now on he will refrain from any acts in that direction."

Aqsaqal looked at me, and added, "but why would I be your speaker, Mikhail? You can speak for yourself. We are among friends here."

Before I could speak, Oleg took out his vibrating phone, whispered something to the president and excused himself from the meeting. I had to say my next words although I didn't want to.

"Yes, it is true that I supported the idea of joining the European community in the beginning of the 2000's. Back then the idea was popular in Russian circles too, which also sought possible closer relations with the EU and considered maybe even joining it. But if my humble activity has been seen as hostile by Russia, I apologise, and will pull my support from the movement and do nothing that could impair Russian interests."

"Ha-ha-ha!" The Puppet Master burst out laughing. "With all due respect, Mr Vorotavich, you have some hubris, I would daresay, young man. How can you, just a businessman, influence Russian interests? Don't take offence, but it's like a mosquito biting an elephant. But you are right in some respects; you would do yourself a favour if you refrain from butting heads with the Bear. You should know your place and stop spreading dubious ideas to the masses."

All of a sudden I had a flashback. The Puppet Master had uttered almost the exact same words as an SBU deputy had twelve years before, when my car had been sprayed with automatic rounds near a Georgian restaurant in Kiev.

The pieces of a grand puzzle started to fall into place inside my mind. It was very likely that this guy had been involved even in the first attempt on my life all those years ago! The Russians had surely paid attention to my political agenda way back at the 2002 elections, and the SBU officer was one of the Puppet Master's men, just as half of the Ukrainian security probably were. I hoped that one day I would have a chance to question, or should I say, interrogate the bastard properly, if only to satisfy my curiosity as to how far back this vendetta went, and how deeply involved the main players were. I understood now what had pissed them off - my propagation of European choice, which had gained a lot of support in Ukraine. Now I saw that I was probably perceived as its initiator! In their eyes I was the source of the *European virus* contaminating much of the Ukrainian population. They might even have thought that I wasn't an independent player and that the United States had prompted Israel, as its close ally, to use me to sever Ukraine from Russia. I had the same mentality as my enemy, so that chain of thought, however bizarre it may sound, wasn't entirely improbable in their minds. Russians always suspect a conspiracy in anything. It was all perfectly clear to me now. I could be wrong, I had no proof, but I trusted my gut feeling.

Oleg re-entered the hall bringing in my mobile phone that I had left with the security downstairs. Wow, fourteen missed calls from an unknown number. What the hell could that mean?

The phone went off again and I answered quickly, looking apologetically around at the others in the room. It was Arthur's voice that greeted me.

"Misha, I just received a phone call giving me a location to pick up Sasha. I'll be there in less than an hour. If I don't call back soon after, it was a trap."

"Be careful, Arthur, and good luck. If all goes well, I'll see you tonight."

"Okay," Arthur agreed, and killed the connection.

Sasha's swift release probably meant to convey two messages: one to stress the power of the Puppet Master in handling things in Moscow and the second, to show reverence towards the Kazakh President and thus emphasize his importance to Russia.

The rest of the meeting was blurred, as my fatigue took a hold of me. I cherished the thought that my brother was safe and it was understood that the president had brokered some kind of unformulated armistice between me and the Puppet Master. Someone wise once said that you make peace with your enemies, not your friends. But this wasn't peace - merely a ceasefire at best with my father-in-law. The truce wouldn't last long, I was certain of that.

Still, as long as it was in place, I would spend some time with my brother. You never really appreciate your relatives when they are around and regret it dearly when they are not. I had an idea. Could anything be better than a few days in the tropics, just me and Sasha? I was already in Asia, so why not treat my beloved brother to a few days in some S.E. Asian paradise.

It's a Brother Thing

My mission in Astana had been accomplished but the visit wasn't over just yet. After I announced that my brother was soon to be freed I accepted congratulations from everyone. I didn't notice where a bottle of champagne suddenly appeared from, but Oleg's crafty hands were already opening it.

I had to thank the Puppet Master for his instantaneous and successful intervention on my behalf, although I had no doubt that it was him who had arranged Sasha's abduction in the first place. But, I needed to follow the rules of pretence and diplomacy. What a fucking hypocrisy to conduct an entire conversation consisting of 90% lies, hinting instead of saying, circumventing instead of being straight to the point. All these things just emphasized the phoney world we were living in.

Finally, the president suggested that I have some rest after my long journey, stating that he had many serious things to discuss with the Russian delegation, as he referred to the Puppet Master this time. I assured everyone of my endless gratitude, bade farewell and left with Oleg.

Oleg insisted that I use his villa to crash instead of going to a hotel. He gave me no choice but to stay the night, as he was organising a banquet dedicated to the miraculous release of my brother and insisted that the hero of the occasion must be present too. Arthur hadn't called me back yet, and my nerves were jangling. I suppressed an urge to call Arthur again. It was the Puppet Master's reputation at stake here after all, if something happened to Sasha before he was safely extracted from Russia. Still, I had to be positive: before fainting or falling asleep, I called my Moscow office, now operating from a temporary location after the main premises were razed to the ground recently by a powerful bomb blast, with orders to arrange for Sasha's transportation to Astana by that evening whether using a charter or a commercial airline. I killed the call, lay back and closed my eyes, and with a smile set on my face, fell into a well-deserved and satisfying sleep.

***

It felt like as soon as my eyes closed I was being manhandled by someone. I awoke with a start to find Sasha's grinning face beaming down at me. The scene took me back some thirty years to when Sasha would try and shake me from my slumber to get ready for school - quickly followed by a slap to the back of the head and a lecture on how I had to study hard and succeed at my studies and that he was the breadwinner now, so I must do as he said. Oh how I had missed him! The few days in captivity hadn't broken him or altered him in any way. He'd obviously had time to change clothes and shave as he looked almost dapper and healthy with his usual look of relaxed self-confidence.

"How's it going, Sleeping Beauty?" Sasha said, huge grin lighting up his face.

I sat up and placed a pillow behind my back. Sasha took my clothes from the chair near the window, threw them on the bed and carried the chair to the bedside. He sat next to me, sipping on some light green drink from a highball, still grinning like the Cheshire cat.

"Hey, give me a sip, I'm really thirsty," I begged enviously.

Sasha rolled his eyes and walked to the small fridge in the corner of the room which I hadn't noticed before I'd fallen asleep. He tossed me a can of Fanta. I picked up my phone, which had half a dozen missed calls, all unanswered because I'd forgotten to take it off silent mode. Arthur would definitely bitch about that when I next saw him.

"That should do you for now," he said.

"So, tell me what happened," I asked, after finishing the ice cold drink in two big gulps.

"I've given all the details, descriptions, scraps of conversations and anything else that may be relevant, to Arthur."

"Now give them to me!"

"Sure, but first I need to know if Yulia and the kids are safe. I asked Arthur and he gave me his usual cold-eyed stare and said I should talk with you. Misha...tell me they are safe."

The question took me by surprise, I had assumed that Arthur would tell Sasha what he wanted to know and put his mind at ease.

"Fucking Arthur...he needs a lesson in how to deal with civilians. Look, Yulia and the children are fine and safe. I didn't want to worry or upset them while I had a chance of saving you. I phoned Yulia and apologised because I had asked you to go to a copper mine in Chukotka on my behalf, as I am not yet in the best shape for such a journey and it was extremely important I am represented by someone I can trust. I told her that you had left immediately, and unfortunately there are no telecommunications possible because of the remote location. I apologised again and said that a car was on its way to take her and the children to a luxury retreat as way of compensation. I promised you would be gone for a week at most. What I would say if you were lost is not something I have thought about too much."

"And she bought your horseshit?"

I shrugged and smiled: "I'm a believable guy."

"An experienced bullshitter, you mean."

"Whatever. It was better than the truth. Which brings me back to my question...tell me everything that happened."

"Okay...in a nutshell, four days ago some paramilitary-type guys, wearing black masks barged into my office. I pressed the security button, but it was too late, as I guess my security had already been dealt with. They held me down and injected something into my arm and I fainted."

Sasha took another sip of his cocktail and looked at something outside the window.

"I came to my senses on a plane. I was tied up with my hands behind my back, alone and blindfolded in some compartment. After a while someone with a mask came in took the blindfold off and gave me some water. After looking around, I could see it wasn't a passenger plane, it was military, of that I am certain. It was still daylight as I could see light through the window. We were already descending and very soon the plane landed. They put the blindfold on again and led me outside. I think it was a very small airport - either private or military, because there was no regular noise of take offs and landings like you would expect to hear. My senses were acute - I could smell the scent of the coniferous trees in the nearby forest, but that was all. Taking into account that we reached Moscow by car rather quickly today, when I was released, I assume we had landed at some military airfield to the north of the Moscow outskirts."

Sasha had a quick search around as he spoke, didn't find an ashtray, so he put his empty glass on the table near him, and lit a cigarette. He opened the window to the outside, took a deep breath, and returned to the chair to finish his account.

"I was held in some kind of detention facility, not a house or something unplanned. The metal door was designed with a small hatch to serve food; there were bars on the window, which was placed high up and way out of my reach. No questions were asked and I didn't see anyone during the days spent in captivity. I figured out that my incarceration was intended to put some pressure on you. Too bad I missed your team playing in the Champions league, eh? I went on the internet on Arthur's phone to see if you were in the news, and the only story connected to you was about Watford winning in the Champions League. And with some style."

Fuck. That was only a couple of days ago, and yet it seemed like centuries had passed. I shook my head at how so much had transpired so quickly.

"Finish your story, Sasha. Your mind wanders like an old woman."

"Oy vey, give me time, little brother. I haven't spoken to anyone in days. It's not like Arthur is the most talkative of your friends, after all."

I chuckled at the thought of Sasha gabbling away in a car with Arthur, with Arthur sat stony faced, ignoring him and wishing he'd shut the fuck up.

"Fair enough...but please...carry on."

"Finally today, my captors unlocked me, put me in a car and drove to some Moscow suburb. We stopped somewhere, and then walked for ten minutes into some woods. Then they freed my hands, took off the blindfold and told me that I was free and that I didn't need to run, as a friend would come to pick me up soon. They turned around and left in no special hurry. I looked around and saw the lights on at the Luzhniki Stadium, which I recognised. That's when I understood that I was in Moscow. I had neither a mobile phone nor wallet on me, so I decided to just wait and see whether someone would show up. Arthur was there in under twenty minutes. He told me that he received an unidentified call and an anonymous person suggested that he come pick me up and gave him my exact location. That's everything, basically. I came here, while Arthur went to Kiev to wait for you there. You were unavailable on the phone, so Arthur contacted David, who told him that your mission in Astana was over and you'd be back soon."

"Sasha, you tell it so nonchalantly; while I was cursing myself that I failed to protect you and that because of me you were in great jeopardy. You act like you didn't break sweat. Although you present it lightly, I know you must've gone crazy in those days, isolated, not seeing a person and wondering what trouble befell you. We need to learn something from this, so nothing so bad can happen again."

Sasha nodded in agreement.

"Listen bro, I have an idea. I have my jet here, and if we have a direct route, we can be in Thailand in something like six hours, just you and me. I know that our wives are waiting and worrying, children are crying and so on, but we need to do it, bro. The fact that Arthur won't be around, makes it even better, as no one will drive us crazy about security and all. We haven't had a proper talk for years, it seems."

Seeing me so passionate, what could Sasha do other than agree. He smiled, and said,

"Thailand? Sounds good, bro!"

"It's agreed then. Once our obligations here are seen to, a little trip, just the two of us."

Sasha left me to get dressed, and I splashed some water on my face and thanked whoever is above us for the safe return of my beloved brother. Shortly afterwards, there was a knock at the door, and in came Oleg.

"Ah, so you are awake! I thought you would sleep through my party for sure. I wanted to ask you something after I showed you the room, and I was only gone two minutes. When I knocked, I could hear you snoring already."

"I think I was more tired than I realised," I said with a smile. "Or maybe just a release of nervous energy after a tense couple of days."

"For sure, Misha. I understand. If my brother was taken..." He let out a huge sigh. "I don't know if I could keep it together like you, my friend. Especially if I came face to face with the person responsible."

"I am sure I will cross swords with the Puppet Monster once more. And sooner, rather than later."

"Indeed, my friend. Anyway, enough business talk. It is time to party. I hope you are refreshed and ready for some decadence, Kazakh style?"

"I was born ready, Oleg. Bring it on!"

***

Once we left Oleg's villa, he outlined his plan for the evening. We were heading to some nightclub, which Oleg reserved in full only for us and his close associates. There would be the usual mix of drinking, strippers and whores, along with a special surprise he had arranged just for me.

"I can't wait, Oleg, I am sure you will surpass all my expectations. But, tell me, have you been back to the palace yet? You could have flown off by helicopter and I wouldn't have heard."

"Yes, I wanted to find out what happened after we left the president and the Russian to chat without us."

"And was there anything interesting?" I enquired, leaning forward in my seat.

"Oh, yeah. Aqsaqal told me that according to all the signs the Puppet Master was really pleased that you were going to abandon your pro-European programs. He never admitted it, of course, but it appears that you had become a real pain in the ass for them at some point."

"That's good. So it sounds like a truce is in place."

"It would appear so," Oleg agreed.

"Listen, man, don't we need to stop by the president's office tomorrow morning? The meeting ended sort of abruptly when we left him with Korablyov, and Aqsaqal hinted at some business I should take a look at."

"Don't worry about that, Misha. At my party tonight, I'll introduce you to Abdi, with whom you'll be in touch regarding the president's programs and commercial interests. Don't worry, he's not from those," Oleg said, putting two fingers on his shoulder, mimicking epaulettes.

This gesture meant that Abdi was not from the secret services, which I was pleased to hear. I'd had enough dealings with spooks to last me several lifetimes.

"He's an economic advisor, very close to Aqsaqal. Good guy. And very bright. And, of course, you have me - your humble servant for anything beyond the regular, like saving your relatives from African cannibals or yourself from jealous mistresses. If you find something interesting in what Abdi would send you, consult me before proceeding. You know, not many investors look into -stan countries, so most of the programs are not too well adapted to financing and securing needs, as most investors expect and prefer."

"Okay, that sounds good. I hope we can get something together that will benefit Kazakhstan as well as myself, but without putting any more targets on my back."

"I'll drink to that!" Sasha joined in, passing Oleg and me a glass of champagne he'd taken from the limo's fridge.

We clinked glasses and put aside talk of business, abductions and conspiracies. I was light-headed after my first glass and getting into the right mood for some kind of Kazakh carnival.

The club was in the city centre. I thought Oleg intended to park the car *inside* the club, considering how close his driver brought us to the entrance. The bouncers opened the car doors for us and we stepped into the club. Everybody knew Oleg and greeted him from all directions. We headed to the VIP area, separated from a main dance floor by both elevation and a low fence.

As we slowly made our way, we were stopped every moment by people saying hello to Oleg. It gave me an opportunity to familiarise myself with the inner decor, which was spacious, with a kind of kitschy style, and it was obvious that the owners had definitely spent some decent money on its hi-tech equipment. It was crammed with lights, screens, special effects and other gimmicks, giving a modern, funky feel in contrast to the first impression. The main bar was in the middle of the floor in the form of square, surrounded on all sides by the main dance floor. Finally, Oleg must have personally greeted everyone in the club, because we made it to the VIP zone. This area was far more plush even than downstairs, and had its own smaller bar. For the first time, I noticed there was a boxing ring on a podium set diagonally across from us.

It appeared that we were the last ones to arrive, as the place was already crowded, with the dance floor heaving, and strippers rotating energetically on the poles in unison with the vibrating music. There were cages suspended from the ceiling and just below us, the balcony was rammed with sexy girls dancing whilst wearing the tiniest dresses. If I got into the right mood I would surely join the girls on the balcony, I thought. When drunk, I don't really have much shame.

A burst of light from the far end of the club caught my attention, and I realised that there was some fakir spitting fire in all directions. It was most unlike any club I'd been to in Kiev or Moscow, but I had to admit that I liked the place.

I wasn't so sure about Sasha though, as he was not usually a partying type. But he was the star of the evening, which was made clear when the music stopped abruptly and someone announced that all guests may now greet the much respected Mr Alexander Vorotavich, who was miraculously freed today from the underworld, in time to join this glamorous party. It looked like everyone in the club, guests and personnel alike, all stood up and started clapping and cheering, all looking in the direction of the VIP area.

I didn't give a fuck about all the fuss, but I knew that Sasha would be uneasy with all the attention. Oleg, in stark contrast, was cheering along with the crowd, and clapping enthusiastically. He slapped Sasha on the back and embraced him, and I got the impression that Oleg was happy for the guests to assume that he had personally freed my brother. It wasn't too far from the truth, so I smiled and clapped and let Oleg bask in the glory. Mercifully, the thumping music started again, the lights dimmed, and everyone went about their business as before - much to the relief of Sasha.

Finally, we reached the massive table that could host maybe thirty of Oleg's closest friends. It was already full except for three chairs at its head. We occupied those seats according to Oleg's instructions and he immediately introduced me to a Kazakh man, who was seated just next to me. This was Abdi, who we had spoken about earlier. He was a tiny oriental man with a long curly moustache in a Genghis Khan style. I gave him my business card and took his in return, while Oleg snatched a bottle from a waiter and began filling his, mine, Sasha's and Abdi's glasses with a white beverage that looked unfamiliar.

"What is that, Oleg?" I wondered, studying the strange potion in my hand. "You drink milk in the clubs here or you've managed to distil cocaine?"

"First you try, after - explanations." Oleg said in a concise club-adapted style with a smile, and held up his drink. We clinked glasses: Oleg, Abdi, Sasha and I, downed it in one, hoping the taste wouldn't be too disgusting.

The shit was strong.

"What the fuck is it, Oleg?"

"You like it?"

"Honestly...it's not bad at all."

"It's *asau kumis* - something Kazakh, man. Very strong like absinth. Did you like it? Answer me before I explain what it's prepared from."

"Well, the taste is interesting. Something a bit sour. What is it - the milk of forty year old Kazakh virgins? But I liked its strength. Few more like these and I'll be wasted, I'm afraid."

Oleg laughed in evil anticipation.

"Oh, you will have many more for sure, my friend. By the way, it's produced from horse milk. I hope that doesn't deter you."

"Don't worry, man. It bothers me less than your determination to get me drunk tonight." I answered, with a wink.

The first glass was already affecting me, so I started to fill my plate quickly hoping I would get some food inside me to soak up the alcohol already in my system. But ruthless Oleg was already pouring us a second glass, citing the traditional drinking proverb that the interval between the first and the second drink shouldn't be long. Bastard. How could I disobey the tradition? Of course, we all downed the second glass promptly. Then, finally I had a chance to bite on something.

"Good! Eat up, Misha," Oleg said, seeing me wolf down some bread and sausage. "You too, Sasha. The night is young, and we have much entertainment for you both."

"What is this?" Sasha asked after chowing down on the sausage.

"Ask your brother," Oleg replied with a laugh. "He ate enough for three people earlier today. Aqsaqal was most surprised that Misha barely left enough for the rest of us."

"Shit...are you serious, Oleg?" I asked with a feeling of dread. The last thing I wanted to do was upset the president.

"I joke with you, Misha. Sasha, it is called *kazy*. It is a special dish made from smoked horse meat. Very special, very expensive."

"Horse meat? Not so different from major chain restaurants, I guess," Sasha said, and bit off another chunk.

As we ate, Oleg mercifully gave us some time between the flow of drinks. As Sasha and I sat back in unison, patting our bellies in appreciation, Oleg stood and beckoned us both over to the balcony, now cleared of the strippers and well positioned in front and above the boxing ring.

"Our president is obsessed with the horses, while my passion is boxing," Oleg explained. "As well as my business interests and official posts, I am also the chairman of the Kazakh Boxing association. I have seventeen boxing clubs under my auspices and we currently have a very promising generation of pugilists. You happened to come on a very special occasion."

Now I understood the backbone of Oleg's *military wing*. Having the entire boxing community under him, no mobster could pose any challenge to him.

Oleg continued in the meanwhile.

"Look, I want to show you one of the prospects that we have here. If he progresses at the same rate as now, I bet he can surpass even the glory of the great Kostya Tsyu eventually."

Below us, the last preparations for the boxing contest were being seen to. The music went silent again and the same voice as before announced the fight between the experienced, former Cruiserweight champion, Alvaro Sanchez from Puerto Rico, versus the unknown local Kazakh guy, having the professional record of only seven fights, but all won by knockout.

I was also a long time boxing fan, ever since befriending my old friend and original partner, Gigo, but I'd never seen a live bout and I must admit, I was getting caught up in the atmosphere of the crowd's excited anticipation. Alvaro was already warming up confidently in his corner, he looked focussed, and oblivious to the partisan support for his opponent. Of course, he was already past his peak, having lost two of his last four fights, but he was still a top five cruiserweight, no doubt about it. The Kazakh guy was then introduced to the cheering cries of the crowd as Aibek Nurislamov. He was very young for a professional boxer; I could tell that much and I didn't envy him having to fight Sanchez. But, the young Kazakh walked calmly and confidently to the ring, seemingly unaware of the fact that he was about to face one of the most experienced veterans in his weight class.

Oleg had long forgotten about me and Sasha, as he cheered and clapped nervously, watching his fighter going through the last formalities before the fight began.

Finally a half-naked girl circled the ring with a number 1 sign and the first round was on. The first few exchanges were dominated by Sanchez, but it was evident already that his younger opponent had much quicker hands. Both fighters were there to fight and didn't clinch much, barraging each other with impressive punch combinations. If I were the referee, I would have awarded the 1st round to the Puerto Rican, although Aibek was able to stun him with a punch or two.

Aibek started the 2nd round far more confidently and took the initiative straight away, backing his opponent to the ropes and unleashing a series of jabs, punctuated with crosses and straight rights. Alvaro was on the defensive most of the round trying to dodge and counter-attack through the flurry of punches from the other side. I started to understand why Oleg had praised this youngster so highly.

The bell rang, and Sanchez looked weary as he went back to his corner and flopped onto his stool. The young Kazakh looked fresh and raring to go, and had to be forced to sit so his corner man could give instructions. In the opening of the third, Aibek managed to floor Alvaro with a brilliant right uppercut to the chin. Alvaro was back on his feet before the count reached five, but should have taken a longer count as it was clear he hadn't fully recovered. Within thirty seconds he was on the canvass again, after taking a jab, cross straight right combination that immediately opened a nasty cut just above his right eyebrow. The referee stopped the fight, saving Sanchez from more serious damage. What a swift and impressive knockout! Sasha and I were cheering and whistling, and Oleg was completely ecstatic, mirroring the crowd, which went crazy. Aibek put his arm around Sanchez, who respectfully raised the young Kazakh's arm in victory, then clapped along with the crowd. The young man bowed respectfully to his opponent, then the crowd, and then looked up at the balcony and bowed especially low to Oleg, who nodded and clapped enthusiastically.

As much as I remember, and it's not much in absolute terms, the decent, restrained part of the night ended shortly after the boxing match. By the fourth or fifth drink I had two Kazakh girls cuddling me like I was some kind of koala. I don't remember asking for them; it was probably Oleg who organised that. What could I do? I'm not that resistant to girls' caresses so I had to enjoy their silky skin and young elastic bodies. By that stage, someone brought some qalyans and chillums and Oleg, who was disappearing and coming back the entire night - probably mingling with the guests as a proud host or shagging someone in the private room, boasted that they were filled with the best hashish from the Chuy Valley or the Valley of Dreams, as it was also known - the most famous marijuana growing district in the entire world. I tried to protest, as I didn't really like to mix drunkenness with being stoned, now that I was a little older, but as with the kumis, Oleg was very persuasive.

As I toked on the chillum, the girls started dancing on our table. A drink or two and another puff later and they pulled me up on to the table to join them. I remember dancing ecstatically to the sounds of rave, feeling a perfect harmony with the music and the universe in general. I was unable to sit anyway, I knew if I sat down, then the *helicopter effect* feeling wasn't far away, and puking would follow close behind.

Eventually I tired of dancing like an old man at a wedding, and so I jumped off the table and collapsed in my chair. The woozy feeling had gone and I needed a break. The girls stepped down too, and the next thing I knew, they had got under the table and were sucking me off one after the other. I didn't care much whether anyone noticed and even less which one of those Asian goddesses took my load in their mouth. As my dick exploded, I lost consciousness in harmony with my orgasm.

When I awoke, I was shocked to discover I was on my own plane, already high in the air, Sasha seated opposite me with a rather gloomy expression. He explained that by the end of the evening I had come to my senses and insisted on going to the airport so we could set off to Thailand. Oleg wasn't certain that it was the right move, but he took us to the airport anyway, as it was impossible to argue with drunken me, stubbornly locked on whatever course of action I was focussed on. He made sure I didn't try to pilot the jet by myself, bade Sasha and me farewell, and ensured that the jet was cleared for takeoff. I must have been pretty fucked up, as I remembered nothing after my under the table dual blow job.

"And how are you, little brother?" Sasha asked once he'd filled me in on my drunken antics. "Well rested?"

"Oh my fucking head."

I winced as I sat up and the banging started, like a pneumatic drill inside my brain.

"Once my hangover subsides, I should call Oleg to make sure I didn't do something extremely obscene last night. What a night though! And a good aperitif for what is to come when we reach Thailand."

Despite my severe hangover, I felt like I could absorb a little more oriental pleasure. And wasn't Thailand just the best place for that?

"Oy vey, he never learns." Sasha said to the heavens as he shook his head.

Full Moon Fun

I couldn't remember telling the pilot where exactly in Thailand to go, but he advised me that he already had clearance to land at Koh Samui airport.

Once we landed, the familiar open air sauna feeling hit us immediately the jet door opened. We stepped onto Thai soil and I smiled at the prospect of a few days of Thai-style relaxation.

"You see - even the airport is stunning!" I remarked to Sasha as he noticed the stylish coconut wood and bamboo arrivals area. We cleared customs and immigration without incident, and I headed into the airport branch of the Siam Commercial Bank and withdrew two hundred thousand baht. Once outside, the throng of locals screaming 'Taxi! Taxi!' 'What hotel you go!' and a multitude of other indecipherable shouts was overwhelming.

"Fuck this," I said to Sasha, "let's get a limo to the pier."

We headed back into the arrivals area and booked a limo for the brief ten minute drive to the pier at Choeng Mon, where the luxury speedboats on offer were a better option to get to our resort on the neighbouring island of Koh Phangan, than the backpacker-laden old fishing boats that left from the nearest pier to the airport. Koh Phangan is a beautiful island in the Gulf of Thailand that held fond memories for me ever since I, along with David and our uni friend, Kobi, had spent a glorious holiday there during our university break, back in the nineties.

The journey took under an hour, and soon enough we were settled in comfortably at the best hotel on Haad Rin Beach. It had been more than fifteen years since I'd been here as a student, and, despite spotting new hotels offering much more classy accommodation in comparison with my last sojourn here, it was still fairly undeveloped and uncommercialised.

As soon as we settled, I hit the mini bar, opened up two Singha's and handed one to Sasha. My hangover was almost gone thanks to the fresh sea air on the speedboat, so it was about time to start refilling the alcohol level in my bloodstream.

"Cheers," I said to Sasha, and clinked bottles.

We walked onto the balcony and sat in the two rattan chairs. The sea was deepest blue, there wasn't a cloud in the sky, so we sat in silent appreciation of our stunning view of the ocean and neighbouring Koh Samui. It was time for quiet observation, letting the relaxed, unhurried atmosphere of Thailand start washing away all the stress of the last few days. The hotel was really luxurious, a stark contrast from my poor student days in Thailand, when we had stayed in a dormitory full of loud, drunken, smelly, farting brit and aussie backpackers.

As I let those memories fill my mind, I gazed out at the water and realised the view wasn't much different from the view I had at my villa in the Cayman Islands.

One huge difference between there and here was that Koh Phangan was a party island, with a massive Full Moon Party every month that drew in over thirty thousand people even in the low season. If you were unlucky, and weren't going to be around long enough for the next one, the kindly locals arranged both half-moon and black moon parties to cover all bases.

Luckily for us - well, me, if I'm honest - the next Full Moon Party was to take place the next day. It would be a perfect way to relive my time on Koh Phangan from so many years before.

"Grab another beer," I asked Sasha as he got up and returned to our room.

"No more Singha," he shouted from inside. "What is this *Chang* beer like?"

"Not so good, if I remember. How about we grab some food and drinks on the beach?"

"Sounds good, Misha. But don't make me eat spicy, okay?"

"Ha ha, as if I would stitch you up, dearest brother."

"Yes...as if."

We headed outside to the beach and walked along the shore until we saw a bar/restaurant that I liked the look of. We sat at a table on the beach and ordered two Singha's whilst we studied the menu.

The waitress brought the beers, and I ordered two *pad thai's* and two banana pancakes to follow. Sasha looked impressed with my grasp of local food, and I didn't have the heart to tell him that on my previous trip, after a bout of the runs, they were the only two dishes I ate for over a week. The waitress returned with our food, placed her hands together in a graceful *wai*, and left us to devour the delicious dish.

"Did I tell you what kind of crazy things I got up to here with Dave and Kobi, when we were here in 1994?"

I thought I had probably recounted my story before, but I wanted to share the memories again. Sasha didn't answer and I wasn't expecting him to, as he had probably tuned in on my mood and was prepared for a monologue on my part.

"There is another small island somewhere near - Orange Island, I think it's called, where I tried my first ecstasy pill. I know drugs don't interest you, and you are right, by the way, I can more than agree after trying most of them, but that was some experience. Something like a first shag, if I look for a proper allegory."

"You are right, I don't like these things. We have a different character after all. You remain romantic of a sort, always eager and open to new experiences, while I have always had to remain focused on mundane, pragmatic things. What are these drugs about? Just a way to escape reality instead of coping with it. That is not my way."

I looked over and saw that Sasha had drunk less than a half of his first beer, while I was rapidly approaching the bottom of my second one.

"Again, you are probably right, Sasha, about drugs specifically, but in a broader sense this life: yours, mine, doesn't matter who's - is too limited time-wise not to try as many things as you can."

I was starting to get philosophic and the beers facilitated my fluency.

"For someone like us, who doesn't really believe in god, what sense do we have in this life? We do things automatically: business, children, vacations, drinks, football without really reflecting on what's important and what's habitual or expected or coerced on us by social norms, colleagues' experiences, TV and other brainwashing things that fill our lives."

I was unable to stop myself. Who else if not my brother, was the perfect audience for my mantra?

"After looking death in the eye, my inner timer is very acute. I almost physically feel the time elapsing each minute, hour, day. I know how abruptly it could all stop. Another sniper waiting for me or explosives attached to my car or an ice pick to my skull, and everything vanishes. Over, just like that." I said with a snap of my fingers. "When you turn forty, it's a real pity to spend life or any part thereof on something secondary. What difference does it make, if I have a million or a billion less or more? Meaningless. I want to spend my time on something grand, on something of value. What's grand you might ask? Something like becoming the richest. Not because of the wealth, per se, but because of the history of winning the competition, of being first to the finish line. Or like saving Ukraine from whatever sinister plans its neighbour might have. But on that, I had to give up any grand plans for Ukraine's future to save you."

I finished my second beer, took the bottle from the stubby cooler and waved it in the waitress' direction. My thoughts were sporadic and scattered or maybe it was still the after-effect of Oleg's lethally strong marijuana?

"Now, what else is important? It's children, because they are gonna rule this world after we are gone. It's also you. You know, bro, when they took you away, I felt like a vacuum. A void spread through me, and I realised that I owed you and myself much more than we've been having together lately, because family is part of us. And it's important any time, not something that should be postponed or overlooked."

Sasha nodded in agreement, and I was pleased he was listening to me, rather than just indulging the rant of a sentimental drunkard.

"Experiences and pleasures are also important. You can view our lives as a bunch of episodes: the more of them positive the happier life you live. The memories all pile up: the first kiss, the first shag, orgy, whatever, they are all engraved in my memory. Many can dwell on their past, but I can't. I can recall something with warmth, but would always try to surpass or at least get more of the same. These are small joys filling our lives. Abstention of any kind is not in my nature."

The waitress brought another Singha and I sipped slowly and continued.

"Nowadays, at my age, I could tell you wholeheartedly, that above meeting your obligations towards the family, like their material support, affording decent living, et cetera, do what you like and quit whatever you don't. Look for yourself, for whatever does good to you. Not much time is given to waste it on something unwanted. Many deceive themselves or sincerely believe that things will get better if they wait, make some efforts and so on. Sometimes it happens, but only rarely. Many end up waiting for better things their entire lives without even trying the things that they were waiting for. What I'm trying to say, is that there is *now* and there is *dare* and these things are important. The past is gone, the future is not guaranteed, so you can plan it, but not rely heavily on having a better life there, while *now* matters the most. *Carpe diem*! Call it obsessive, but I didn't want to wait on our quality time together even a single day."

I exhaled, relieved I had finished my rant, and it had mostly made sense.

"You know, Sasha, daring or chutzpah is probably one of the most inherent Jewish character traits. It is the one for which we are being hated so much by so many in this world and admired by many others simultaneously. The other one is probably instinct for commerce. Take for example what happened all those years ago at Entebbe Airport."

"The hostage thing?"

"Yes. Who else would dare to imitate the Ugandan President's car and escort, bring it over to Uganda from Israel on a military plane and under such a disguise, storm the hijacked plane and release the hostages before the terrorists could understand what was going on? Or who would dare to steal three military vessels from a French port because France refused supplies because of an embargo? Can you imagine anyone else doing that? But, let's leave military operations aside. Take Einstein, for example. Apparently he was kicked out of school or uni at some stage, so he worked on his own and came up with his relativity theory, thus negating and undermining the entire long-known Newtonian mechanics. We just never take no at its face value. And I have come to believe that it is the right approach."

Sasha took out a Camel cigarette, stuck it between his lips and lit it. The breeze herded the cigarette smoke cloud towards me and I inhaled, remembering nostalgically my smoking period. This was definitely a *smoking moment*, but I resisted the urge to join him.

Sasha took a couple of deep drags, then leaned towards me.

"Well, Misha, I think you have a somewhat fatalistic approach, but I guess it has resulted from your own experiences. I can understand your perspective as someone who has nearly died a couple of times, as well as someone who wanted to escape the shackles of poverty. My vision is far simpler. I don't chase things: not money, nor glory, nor adventures, or novelty. We've achieved a certain level of prosperity. Yours is high compared to mine, yet I'm completely content with my place in this world. Your life experience is vast with all the assassination attempts, politics, victories, defeats and many other peaks and pits, while mine is much narrower. You are a gambler of a sort, constantly willing to risk what you've achieved in order to achieve more, while I don't think I need more than I already have. I don't think there is a recipe for a life path unless someone believes in whatever their religion postulates, so one should go with his instincts, inner belief, or sense of accomplishment."

Sasha was getting philosophic too, even before I fetched some grass from the more remote parts of Koh Phangan.

"But we definitely need to hook up more frequently. They don't need to kidnap me or anyone for that matter."

We both sat back, happy that we'd said our individual pieces, and the philosophical vibe slowly ebbed away. The waitress brought our banana pancakes and we sat and ate in silence.

"You want to hit the beach? Go for a swim?"

"No, I think I'll wait till tomorrow."

"How about we find some English, European bum who will sell us some stuff?" I offered, knowing that Sasha would tut and shake his head.

"Tell me more about your first time here. Your voice sends me to sleep." Sasha joked.

I took him up on the invitation though, and continued my account of the mischief's I had on the island with Dave and Kobi. I told Sasha how Dave was on a constant search for something narcotic, swallowing anything claimed to have any psychotropic effect, and unfortunately most of the stuff he purchased was fake.

I then told him how Kobi used condoms even when just sitting in the bath tub with a local bar girl, scared to death he'd catch HIV otherwise. And how David shagged a ladyboy by mistake during the Full Moon Party and Kobi, after hearing about David's encounter, ended up being chased down the beach by a group of angry bar girls because he kept trying to force his hand in their panties to check for a cock.

"Ha-ha-ha, just like Frank Begbie in the *Trainspotting* movie, discovering a dick while supposedly making out with a chick in the car, huh? That must've been hilarious," Sasha burst out laughing as he pictured the scene in his imagination.

"The final indignity was that when we returned to our dorm the following afternoon, still drunk, stoned and coming down from some pills, and discovered that someone had robbed us of our cash and possessions. It was a crappy ending to an unforgettable couple of weeks, but in the following years I would always think back to my time on this paradise island with a smile on my face."

We paid the bill and headed back to our room, where we sat once more on the balcony until the sun set. A glorious red and orange glow spread over the sea and streaked the sky, before shrinking and disappearing over the horizon, chasing after the sun.

We chatted about old times - our childhood, our father being taken away, our cousin Tolik, who perished in Chechnya, anything and everything that came to mind. It was great to feel free of time and the pressures we were usually immersed in. It was exactly what I wanted from this trip - the unlimited opportunity for me and Sasha to sit and talk and feel together again. After finishing the pack of beers we'd brought in from the local 7/11 store, I headed to the shower and stood under the scalding water, letting the past few days stresses wash away. I came out just as Sasha headed off to swim in the sea. He said he wanted to swim, then shower and relax in front of the television, so I decided to venture out to see what was up on the Full Moon Party's eve.

***

With the fancy clothes I was wearing, I attracted a lot of attention from the bar girls as I wandered along the main strip. The cries of *'hansum man, you want party?'* followed in my wake as I checked out my surroundings. I desperately wanted to procure a couple of joints from the backpackers, but I knew my appearance would raise suspicions if I looked like an aging millionaire. I had to blend with the crowd, so I headed into the first clothes store I saw and bought a pair of linen shorts and a t-shirt with two Thai elephants on it. I thanked the seller with 'kawp khun ka' - the only Thai phrase I remembered, and the girl laughed and said,

"You speak like lady!"

She then tried to explain that I should say 'khrap' at the end of a sentence - 'ka' was for ladies. Oh well, I thought my memory had served me well! Besides, saying something very similar to 'crap' when meaning 'thank you' sounded weird.

Nonetheless I said *kawp khun khrap* to the pretty shop assistant to make her happy, and left the store feeling much better wearing my new outfit. The disguise would downgrade me sufficiently from my white slacks and light blue button-down shirt, which just didn't look counterfeit enough to pass for a local *replica* of a famous brand.

As far as I remembered, getting hold of some weed wouldn't be complicated on Koh Phangan. Probably eighty percent of backpackers had it, some sold it, some offered a wider range of stuff, and everyone knew where to get it. The island was already crowded in anticipation of the upcoming Full Moon Party, so when I left the strip and headed on to the beach, it was hard to make my way through the heaving masses of party people, mixed with a tiny minority of locals wearing leather jackets and jeans in the incredibly hot weather. These were rumoured to be cops masquerading as *Thai mafia*, arriving on the island for their Full Moon sweep of drug dealers. Although every now and then, some poor cunts were caught red-handed, the rumour mill speculated that only dealers who refused to pay a bribe were targeted.

The beach and its bars were already packed with revellers, most of whom were much younger than me, probably on a gap year to the Far East. I envied them their youth, although they would probably envy me too, if they saw my private jet or bank account statement. But I couldn't buy my youth back, so they had something that my wealth couldn't buy. But I could try to feel the same way again, so, I hit a beach bar, barely able to reach the counter through the rows of people. I put my sunglasses on and dishevelled my hair, hoping that no one would recognise me as the owner of Watford United. After a couple of joint cheers and general small talk with two chicks who were hanging out with a young lad, I felt acquainted enough to ask whether they knew where to get a couple of joints. After measuring me up from head to toe, the lad pointed to a table at the far end of the bar and suggested that Sam, the guy with dreadlocks might have something for me.

"The one who looks like a drug dealer?" I joked lamely, but they didn't return my smile.

With the Sam guy, whose real name was probably Ernesto or Guido, judging from his Latino look, it was a quick business. We stood up, walked down the side of the bar into a dark alley and he passed me a small bag which smelled potent enough to my nose for me to be sure I wasn't being ripped off. I handed him a two hundred euro bill and told him to keep the change, which was very generous on my part, but I was just happy to have scored so quickly and easily. I thought he'd be happy, but he immediately suspected that I had given him a counterfeit banknote. Drug dealers are very sceptical characters and he found it hard to believe someone would pay him more than twice the price. Reminiscing back to my little foray into dealing when I was a student, I could understand his distrust. Seeing him so worried, I gave him five thousand baht instead, a bit more than he wanted and much less than I'd intended originally. I smiled and thanked Sam, then continued down the alley to the road, and headed to my room to have a puff. I didn't like weed that much, but if I didn't smoke at least one joint on Koh Phangan, it would be like visiting Ukraine without tasting a borsht.

Sasha was already asleep when I returned, so I rolled a joint on the balcony and relaxed in a rattan chair. The sound of thumping music from just up the beach was too much temptation, so after stubbing out the joint, I went back to the main strip to find somewhere to drink. I hooked up with two young Russian chicks in a bar, who fully intended to party through the night and continue on into the Full Moon Party. Seeing that I was no match for either of them in their endeavour, I paid the bill, bought them a bottle of Champagne and let them be, hoping that if I ran into them the next evening they might remember my kind gesture.

**

I woke up refreshed, relaxed and worriless for the first time in what seemed like weeks, but in reality were just a few days. As soon as I recalled that it was the Full Moon Party day, I felt almost euphoric! Things were definitely taking a turn for the better. Looking at my smart phone, I noticed that the number of missed calls had risen to twenty six. Shit, I must've slept at least twelve hours. Such a lengthy and restful sleep hadn't happened much lately, except for my coma, of course.

Sasha's day, in contrast, was already half way through. He had eaten breakfast, been swimming in the sea, dived for an hour after renting some gear from one of the numerous shops on the beach, and was already going through the hotel menu, planning his lunch. I told him to order some coffee for the room, and said I would join him after I'd showered and dressed.

We sat on the balcony watching the endless throng of boats coming from all directions and disembarking more and more people right on the beach. The buzz on the island was growing in anticipation, and numerous bars were playing loud rave and trance for the mass of young travellers who had started to party already.

I was in no hurry. Remembering being completely lost almost twenty years before in similar circumstances, I intended on being more cautious this time. With age comes wisdom. I went through the missed calls to see if there were more than two or three calls from the same number, hinting at something urgent. There was nothing of the kind. Even Masha had called only once.

I called her back, letting Sasha add few words of his own too. I hoped that Sasha's presence, whom my wife treated as much more restrained and responsible man than me, would give our spontaneous getaway a bit less of an unruly air.

The room attendant knocked and brought in our food, and we continued watching the chaotic scene below. The sun was already going down, reminding me that I'd slept through most of the day. The music volume increased as more and more bars added to the cacophony, and with a full stomach, it was time to get in the party mood.

"Shall we take a look around?" I asked Sasha, glancing down at the beach below us.

"Why not? I am interested to experience some of this Full Moon - but don't expect me to be your wingman all night."

"Of course. Let's check it out, brother."

We wandered down to the fledgling party and stopped at one of the more empty beach bars for a warm up drink. Since I'd been having too many beers during the past few days, my body was already accustomed and I knew it would take many bottles to get me drunk, so I switched to vodka to jumpstart my party spirit. Even Sasha agreed to have a couple of shots with me, although he was going to enjoy the festival more as a spectator rather than a full participant. He beckoned to an old lady walking the beach, looking for a client to give a foot massage. Well, anyone should enjoy what they like. She pointed to a small sala near the alley that led to our hotel, and led Sasha away, not before I left my most valuable belongings with him, so they wouldn't be pick pocketed.

There were already several thousand partygoers dancing and drinking and the evening hadn't fully started yet. I bar-hopped, looking for a spot where I could observe the evening's festivities, and eventually I bumped into the Russian chicks from the previous night. They seemed full of energy despite partying through from the previous night. It was either the twenty years age difference between us or they had scored some coke or speed.

While Sveta was a regular Slavic chick from Saratov, cute and sexy, her friend Oxana had Uzbek in her, and her oriental roots could easily make her pass for a local Thai bird. I wondered whether she was getting propositioned all the time by elderly sex tourists treating her as a Thai prostitute. I hung out with them mostly, rarely able to keep up with their energetic dancing. Thankfully, Sasha wandered into the bar and took a table near us, so I had an excuse to sit for a while and catch my breath. The girls joined us, and I could tell immediately that Sveta made a good impression on Sasha, so I gave all my attention to Oxana.

A few drinks later, and Oxana agreed to go to my room, just for a joint, of course. I told Sasha we wouldn't be too long, and he nodded, smiling in a way that I knew meant he didn't believe me. We hurried to the hotel, sat on the balcony so we could enjoy the party unfolding below, and I rolled a fat joint. I suggested we went inside to enjoy the air con while we had a beer to accompany the weed, and once inside I made my move. With very little prompting, we got naked and played with each other, but I thought I'd been knocked back when Oxana didn't want me on top of her.

"What's wrong?" I asked softly, hoping I would at least get a blow job still.

"It's the beginning of my period," she whispered. "You can do me in the arse though, if you like. The Full Moon Party would be imperfect, if I don't get laid in one way or another. Why not try something exotic?" she smiled sultrily.

Wow, I liked the spirit! This younger generation was crazy! Most girls freak out when you are near their anus, and this young chick was offering it up like a hand job. How could I say no? That would be impolite.

Although she looked Thai, mentality wise there was no resemblance. Contrary to the mild and amorphous attitude of the Thai chicks, Oxana was a real tigress sucking up all my energy in our aggressive, loud sex session.

She came, I came, but the consequences were drastically different for each of us. She seemed even more vibrant afterwards, while I was barely able to move. She took a quick shower and left to rejoin the party, while I laid still for an hour or two and only then mustered enough energy to head back out.

I found Sasha and let him know that if he fancied that Sveta bird, I didn't think it would require much persuasion to get into her panties. Sasha seemed attentive to the idea. The boats were still spilling newcomers on to the beach, where tens of thousands of revellers were already partying hard. Nobody tried to hide if they were smoking a joint anymore, the pills and acid tabs were passed around and swallowed in the open by the dancing hedonistic crowd. The music volume seemed to increase even more, and I wondered whether I had swallowed something accidentally, because even the sea appeared to be dancing harmoniously with the rave music waves. It was how I imagined the last days of Pompeii - it was anarchic and apocalyptic, as any such event should be, as if there was no tomorrow.

While I was pouring another shot, coming to the conclusion that it might be the last one, Sasha handed me my ringing mobile phone. I answered on autopilot, spotting a Swiss number and wondering who the fuck would want me now.

"Hey Misha, it's Josef, I've been trying to reach you for a couple of days now."

I heard him too well, allowing for the thunderous music around. Shit, I'd pressed the speaker button accidentally. Josef was my personal wealth manager at the Credit Bank of Geneva.

That part of my life seemed so remote to me as I sat in a bar in Thailand in the middle of such a wild gathering. I regretted taking the call and was determined to disconnect as quickly as possible.

"Hey, Josef, it's really late. Oh shit, right, you are calling from Europe, it must be noon time. Anyway, what's up, something's urgent?"

"No, nothing urgent, Misha," Josef said, hearing the ambience around me, and probably regretting calling me with something minor. "I just needed your instructions on what to do with $500,000 US dollars that arrived in your account for the sale of 1,345,000 shares in Neplokho Energy."

No matter how drunk and stoned I felt, I was still dumbfounded with what he was saying. I looked at the phone for a second to make sure I was really engaged in a telephone conversation and not hallucinating. The call was on. What the hell was Josef talking about?

"Josef, are you delirious or what? 1.3 million shares is my entire stock in Neplokho Energy and that stock is worth 15 billion US dollars, grosso modo. How the fuck did you arrive at the conclusion that I sold my stock? Five hundred grand is what? Something that my mother gives me for pocket money for school, *blyad*."

Josef was a really a nice guy, I shouldn't have been so rude with him, but the bullshit he was spouting was too much for me.

"Misha, Misha, I'm so sorry. Please, calm down. It must be some kind of mistake. I've taken it right from the payment reference that came with the deposit. Here, I've opened it in the meantime, that's exactly what it says: 'final payment for

1,345,000 shares in Open Joint Stock Company Neplokho Energy.' It all looks legit, Misha."

Suddenly, for me the party was over! I was sober instantaneously, like from a big line of sniff, but without the pleasant after effects. I ruthlessly disconnected Josef, fearing that otherwise I might electrocute him over the phone for being the messenger of such news.

I had a sense for these things. It was no fucking mistake, I had been robbed at the Full Moon Party again! But this time it wasn't a few thousand baht, but fifteen billion green crunchy US dollars - probably the biggest robbery in history. The major part of my fortune was gone!

Only twenty minutes before, the calls from outside seemed so alien to my partying mood, now, I felt exactly the opposite, my mind already jumped to Europe, trying to form a course of action.

"What is wrong, little brother? You look as white as a ghost."

"The party is over, Sasha."

I told Sasha to get ready to leave soon and went back to the room to make a few phone calls while it was still day time in Europe. Ruining a Full Moon Party for me was just about second to kidnapping my brother in my book of malfeasance, and whoever did it would pay for sure. Once again I was events driven and not the other way around. I would find the son of a bitch responsible, and when I did, I might ask my new *friend* - the Puppet Master to show me a new technique or two on how to do someone in.

Double Betrayal

My flight crew were probably having their sweetest wet dreams when I woke them up and told them to be prepared for the soonest possible takeoff. The party was ruined and so was my assumption that I'd neutralized the most immediate threat to me by appeasing the Puppet Master. The Puppet Master wasn't after the money, of that I was sure. Money didn't interest him, so it had to be someone else.

It was a couple of hours before we were cleared to leave, during which time I turned my work area into a war room so I would have every question prepared when I got to Kiev. I called everyone who I could ask for help, give instructions to or wanted to be involved in finding out what was going on. My satellite phone was in constant use during the flight back to Europe, so whoever is responsible for such things would probably need to launch another sat soon with all the traffic that I was giving them.

I re-qualified Vera from stewardess to my in-flight secretary and put her in front of me with a legal pad perched on her knees prepared to take notes. Two pages were soon covered with numbers, notes, names and dates. I checked my online banking statements and noticed that there were quite a few unexplainable entries. Weirdly though, they were mainly incomes, but I didn't believe someone was just donating money to me. Obviously, whoever credited my account had received something in return of an incomparably higher value than the modest amounts on the screen in front of me.

The sale of shares couldn't have gone unnoticed. We were talking about a public company, after all. Eventually I got around to calling Boris, ready for his take on the raid on my company.

"Ah, here you are, Misha. You know we've been looking for you for quite some time," Boris said when the connection was made.

"Listen, man, you can save the smartass comments for later and make as many jokes as you like, but first I need you to look into the sale of shares of Neplokho Energy, I got a call..."

"Misha, I don't need to inquire into anything," Boris interrupted me rudely. "That's exactly what I wanted to update you about. Your fucking American pederast banker Johnny has been having some fun selling different shares of the group to unknown off-shore entities, while you were in a coma."

"What??!!"

I thought the force of my rage would plunge the plane downwards.

"That's a fucking breach of trust."

If my plane had rockets with nuclear warheads, I wouldn't have hesitated to fire one at Johnny.

"Sure. You tell him that, when you see him, Misha," Boris continued caustically. "This motherfucker alienated shares in six more companies, all using different Powers of Attorneys issued in his name in the past, and conveying some bearer shares that were in his custody. From what I've discovered, he disappeared the moment he found out that you're back with us from your coma. Arthur's actively seeking his whereabouts and he went to Kishinev as soon as he came back from Moscow. He's expected to be back tomorrow. David is afraid to speak to you, Misha. Don't be too hard on him. It's not his fault, but he feels guilty that he recommended Johnny in the first place."

I was speechless, struggling to regain control of myself as the red mist descended. The whole chain of transactions appeared to begin around the time I took a sniper's bullet to the head. Coincidence?

"Where and how did Johnny do the sales?" I wanted to have precise information. "And who are the acquirers?"

"We are still in the process of collecting all the info, but it seems that at least some of the sales were done through a notary in Geneva, which is not unsurprising because of the nature of the deals. We already have some copies, and all of them have the signature of John Wiseman, acting as an attorney for your holding companies."

"Revoke all the fucking Powers of Attorney ever issued to him." I knew it was too late and it wouldn't change anything now. "And find him. That's the most important task for now. At least in Ukraine we should to be able to find all the loose ends and see where they lead."

"I'm on it." Boris said, the sarcastic tone no longer evident.

I disconnected and sat back into my seat in a daze. How come this guy, who was practically under my nose all the time, afraid of just about everything, got involved in something that required some nerve and guts? The Powers of Attorney were issued to him under my instruction, because he was responsible for corporate structuring aimed at securing minimal taxation and maximum impenetrability. And after all these precautions, Johnny - the insider whom I feared the least, makes a move and grabs my shares? I'd despised his cowardly attitude for years and yet he turned out to be the one to defy me. He knew who I was and that I would never let him get away with something like that. Well, I was in a coma, so he might've assumed that I wasn't gonna be around any time soon. But still, the entire scheme was too brave for Johnny. There must be someone else involved in it too! My confidence in that theory grew with each minute that passed. I couldn't have been so wrong about him, although I had to admit I wasn't that good with understanding the American mentality as I was the Soviet. He could only have undertaken those actions out of a greater fear than the fear of my revenge, I thought. The jet would soon be landing in Kiev, and I couldn't wait to hear what Arthur had discovered through his many contacts.

＊

Arthur was already waiting for me at the airport, and he was pissed with me for some reason. What was that all about, god damn it? I'm gone for less than two days on vacation and everyone treats me as if I neglected them for years. What's wrong with them all? With Arthur I was sure that I would know right off, as he never took any kind of a delicate approach to anything.

"Arthur, good to see you. You have the latest update on this situation?" I said in a friendly manner, ignoring his angry scowl.

Arthur didn't smile.

"Misha, you go to Kazakhstan unguarded, then you don't answer my calls when I have Sasha. You are far away, with the Puppet Master in the same city. Then you skip any security and run away to Thailand, like you did when you were twenty something to the Kazantip trance festival. But you aren't twenty anymore and the situation is different. The peril has not subsided because you've sorted something out with the Puppet Master. He's the most formidable of all your rivals, but for him you are just a negligible nuisance. However for the handsome trio of the Chechen Ruslan Sanayev, your friend Denis Filatov and American Johnny, you are the most feared and omnipotent opponent and they would do anything to get rid of you."

Wow, I must've really stepped on Arthur's toes to provoke such a long lecture from this usually laconic character. I don't think he had ever spoken so bluntly to me before, so I guess he had good reason.

"But haven't you yourself told David and Boris, that the Puppet Master is the prime adversary and all the rest play a secondary role?"

I wanted to make some order for my own understanding of the collective of deadly *admirers*.

"Don't get me wrong, only the Puppet Master belongs to a league higher than ours and having him out of the way should make the things easier, but the others do pose very clear dangers that we need to deal with."

I considered Arthur's words, and had to agree that he was correct in his summation.

"You are right, Arthur, you stay by my side now. I'm not gonna run away unguarded anymore. And what's with Johnny, did you find him? Can I come strangle him somewhere?"

"We found out that Johnny wasn't exactly satisfied with the role that he played in your managerial board. After questioning his maid, colleagues in the American community here in Ukraine and collecting some other circumstantial evidence, the picture is clear that he was sure that you'd made many blunders and that he thought of himself as a much better manager than you. He complained about that, not in these words, of course, even to David a few times. His pique grew and was brewing, requiring release. At some stage he got friendly with your so-called friend, Denis, who he knew before he left our group and became a notable independent businessman."

I'd missed this change in Johnny, but now that Arthur was laying it out, he was probably right in retrospect. Now I recalled that Johnny did try to convince me to pay more attention to the opportunities the insurance business offered and some other stuff that I waved off. Was that enough for him to turn traitor?

Arthur continued his emotionless account of his findings.

"After the assassination attempt, I put heavy surveillance on Denis, because I suspected that his invitation for me to come train his security and therefore leaving you with others when the shot was taken, wasn't just a coincidence. I think that Denis, or more precisely his security, realised that he was being followed, because they changed route a few times in contrary to the dossier I prepared. Nevertheless, I've managed to assemble a puzzle from the different pieces of information and intercepted calls. The details are less important, but the bottom line, which has high probability of being correct, is that Denis somehow exploited John's resentment of you and when he did a thing or two that wasn't in line with your expectations, Denis took Johnny by the throat and blackmailed him, probably with just the threat that if he didn't do what Denis asked, he would turn him in to me and David. The conclusions are quite grounded. Johnny is a coward, it wouldn't have taken much."

My list of people to get squared with was expanding. I knew that Denis coveted my business, and he'd found a loophole to attack through.

"Now, once you came around, John was probably feeling that he was completely cornered between you and Denis, afraid of both of you. He alone didn't have the guts for this, but it was too late to try to make amends. John must've been in a panic, and probably understood that now that you were recovered, he was doomed. The employees I've questioned mentioned specific interest that Johnny expressed in stories about your attitude towards traitors before he disappeared. He sent out his family by regular airline, while he himself was afraid to cross the border officially, suspecting that Denis, for sure, and maybe we too were watching his movements. John was obviously scared to death from what he did and was sure there would be immediate retribution. You won't believe what an escape route he chose."

"By now I would believe anything, Arthur. You fire away. What, he crawled into a railway diesel wagon heading abroad and travelled immersed in the oil all the way? Or rented a donkey and found some path in the Carpathian Mountains to cross over to Romania like Sancho Panza?"

"Not quite, but close." Arthur didn't react to my black humour. The only time I'd ever seen him smiling was when he cut off the bandit Nazar's fingers on my request.

"He found a drunkard, retired pilot, who agreed to take him on an old An-2 prop plane - a Kukuruznik used by a local skydiving club, over to Moldova. I found the pilot and interrogated him, he said that if he knew the guy was afraid of flying he would never have taken him. As you know, Kukuruznik's are not the most stable or aerodynamic planes, and are very susceptible to turbulence. The pilot said that his passenger was hysterical for most of the journey. He vomited, prayed loudly in some foreign tongue, ran around the cabin, and finally grabbed the pilot's hand, begging him to land immediately."

"Ha ha, that sounds like Johnny all right. This Kukuruznik probably makes more distance vertically falling into every pit and climbing back on course, than flying forward. What did the pilot do? Find a closer airstrip?"

"No, the pilot turned round, punched the traitor squarely on the jaw and knocked him out. The pilot remembered that when he brought Johnny round once they were in Moldova his entire hair was grey and he wasn't able to stop stuttering. I lost track of Johnny at that point, but I will find him. The head of the counter-intelligence department there is my old friend from the army and he promised to ask his colleagues to determine which way he headed after Kishinev."

"He must've been terrified indeed to undergo his worst nightmare to get away from Ukraine. And rightfully so, because I'm gonna break him limb by limb when I get my hands on the lousy bastard."

Now I wanted to focus on his operator.

"Okay, we'll await news from your friend, Arthur, we need this stuttering motherfucker captured and after he undoes what he did, have him hung on the main square in Kiev as a warning to others. Now, what about Denis? Is he waiting for a duel with me at some forest with his seconds?"

"Denis feels smug these days. He managed to avert the threat from the president's family and to side with them somehow. He feels he can confront you in the open now, and from the entire number of seven company stakes sold by Johnny at least some have been sold to the president's family. At Ukraine Metallum they've summoned a general shareholders' meeting, scheduled for October 13th. At the insurance company the new manager was appointed by a new shareholder's decision and took over the company with the help of the police. The officer in charge, who I know, referred to a direct order from at least the minister's level or even higher."

I shook my head at the news that a whole band of conspirators seemed to be aligning against me.

"You seem to be full of good news. Listen Arthur, before I forget, Boris had some minor shares in Ukraine Metallum, so let's try to use that as leverage to postpone the meeting. In the meantime, all minor assets of Metallum should be transferred to a new company. Such a deal would be, of course, voidable in court, but if I regain control over our steel holding, I can take care of my assets' safe return, and if not - let them chase the assets, like I'd be chasing the shares. I'll talk with Boris about it, but he will need your help and support."

These were minor tactical moves, even acts of despair designed purely as a time wasting move, but it was the most I could do, given the circumstances.

For something more significant and permanent, I had to find out who the purchasers were and challenge the transactions under which they acquired the shares, to find this *blyad* Johnny and take an affidavit from him that he was acting under coercion, or to coerce him, if necessary, to give me a *coercion affidavit*. Most importantly, I had to reconcile all loose ends with the *Family* - the notorious and limited circle of businessmen, officials and individuals, who had formal, informal and relative relations with the incumbent Ukrainian president - Georgiy Nechiporenko. The Family basically ran the country, took a huge share of its budget and performed the majority of the hostile takeovers under the president's auspices. Without the Family's sanction no one would've dared to mess with me.

I thought I was a part of the Family too, but it seemed that a relative in a coma was swiftly replaced by another more apt individual, and once Denis was in, my return to the Family's warm embrace was impossible.

Realising the full scale of the personal and business attacks, all orchestrated and timed with such precision, I didn't feel so comfortable in my own office and in my home town. I gazed out of the window, but instead of drawing energy and confidence from the magnificent view of the Dnieper River I warily scrutinised every bus, taxi, minivan or SUV, wondering whether it was bringing the assault squad to storm my compound. Then I stepped back and closed the blinds, realising I was presenting myself as a target for any sniper that might be waiting for an opportunity to strike. Kiev wasn't safe for me again! I lacked the political backing of the establishment, and who, if not Boris, was the most likely to restore it?

***

I accompanied Arthur to the door and saw Boris was already waiting for me in the reception room, not willing to interfere while I was in a meeting with Arthur. That was strange, it wasn't in line with Boris's usual arrogant and tactless behaviour. Something was wrong with him too, I could tell. Seeing him stooping and hesitant was a shock, and for the first time I realised that I hadn't seen him since my brain took a bullet. How much could someone change in a little over a month?

Above the guest sofa, where Boris sat waiting, was some artwork drawn by a young Ukrainian artist, which I had bought at Andriivskiy, the largest open air gallery for artists in Kiev. I liked to look at it from time to time, so I put it where I thought it was harmonious with the colours and atmosphere of a waiting place. The painting was dedicated to the siege of Kiev by the Mongolian hordes and I, and probably everyone else, became a bit tenser when looking at it before entering my office. I felt I was also currently under siege, and the painting was perfectly attuned with my current state of affairs.

I beckoned Boris in, frowning at the sight of him waiting patiently on the sofa for my audience.

"What's up, Boris? You think I woke up as a vampire or something? I'm not used to seeing you politely waiting for me in reception."

I was counting on Boris' connections and abilities more than the brutal force of Arthur. I needed him to snap out of the stupor he was in.

"What's the matter? We haven't seen each other since I left the hospital, man."

"I'm sorry. I have something I need to say, so hear me out. "

"Okay, " I said, my curiosity pricked. "Go ahead."

"You know, Misha, when you were in the coma, the situation was eating me from the inside - the thought that you might not wake up before I had a chance to tell you this."

Boris had grabbed my attention alright. I intended to send him straight to the president to try to persuade him that somebody was manipulating the opinion of his people against me, but now I had to give Boris the chance to speak about what was on his mind. He seemed too shaken anyway, to perform any immediate task. He brought the chair closer to my desk and not daring to look me in the eye, he started to talk.

"You know, Misha, you've made me. I'm much older than you are, but I must admit, that were it not for you, I would have probably become a modest retiree somewhere in Chernigov area. But it took me time to develop my loyalty to you. At first, I was glad that you left me to manage Azov Oil and Gas Company, but I was sure that I was holding it on borrowed time and soon you would replace me with someone closer to you."

I sat in silence, drumming my fingers on the table impatiently, but wasn't willing to interrupt Boris yet. Boris took another breath and continued his monologue.

"At first, I was acting like every bureaucrat in this country. I inflated the bribes that I gave to all kind of officials, putting the difference into my pocket; I got kickbacks from our suppliers and subcontractors and sometimes sold our produce for a lower price because of personal incentives from our buyers. I mean, I stopped all of that many years ago, when we became friends and you weren't just my boss anymore. You know, I don't have a family of my own and I've always treated you like a son, so when you were shot, the idea that I wasn't loyal to you at some point sat heavily on my consciousness. My torment surprised me, I didn't even think I had one. You know that I'm as callous as a rhinoceros and usually don't give a fuck about the filth that we live in, but in your case I couldn't keep it inside myself anymore." He went silent, and then added: "Any punishment that you choose is appropriate in my case."

Why did he tell me all this? Fuck, I didn't want to know about what defects my friends have. Ignorance is sometimes better. I stared at Boris, not letting any of my facial muscles betray the rage simmering within me. Punishment, he said? I'd give him one.

"You know, Boris, I call that a betrayal. I'm sure, you call that betrayal too. And you know what punishment treason deserves? However, I see that your remorse is sincere, and I don't want to punish you, but I can't just waive it. It wouldn't be right."

I truly felt that I didn't have a choice.

"I have an idea. I can forgive, for sure, but let fate decide your destiny. Or the Lord, if you believe in him."

I opened the desk drawer and took out a revolver, which ironically, given the circumstances, had been a gift from Denis. I emptied five rounds, leaving the sixth inside and then spun the cylinder, enjoying the touch of the cool metal. It always felt good, even natural to hold a gun in my hand.

Boris understood my idea and was trembling in anticipation. Reluctant to part with the weapon, I nevertheless handed him the revolver, afraid for a split second that he might use it on me. I held on to the weapon as he took it, and held his gaze. The torment was evident in his eyes. He blinked, nodded, and then looked at the weapon.

Boris pointed the revolver at his temple. I was cold and resolute, hypnotised by this Russian roulette scene and believing that it was a good solution. If the blood splattered, that's his destiny, and if not, I'm going to embrace him. But let's see if he has the courage first.

He looked up, his eyes now displaying only sadness. He tried to mumble something to me, but the words didn't come out. Boris pulled the trigger, and a dry *click* sound followed. It was empty, nothing happened.

Boris slumped in his chair. I don't know if he fainted or maybe had a heart attack, but I pressed the secretary button to tell her to bring in some water fast. I picked up the revolver that had slipped from Boris' grip and fallen to the floor, aimed at a huge floor vase in the corner of the office and pulled the trigger.

BOOM! The next chamber was loaded. The vase shattered into a thousand pieces, spraying Olga - my secretary, who was just entering with the tray and a glass pitcher on it. She dropped the tray and the pitcher and fainted too.

Two unconscious people and everything covered with debris - I was pleased with this opportunity to release some steam. As staff entered the office and security rushed in response to the gunshot sound, I tried to conceal the grin that was trying to spread over my face.

Svetlana - my personal assistant, entered, and being used to my eccentric behaviour, ignored the mess and told me calmly that someone from Huberman Real Estate Agency in New York was waiting for me on line two. That was the CIA, as Huberman was their agreed cover when calling. I'd had a meeting with them just recently, where we agreed to keep in touch and exchange information on three subjects: threats posed to me personally, developments in Ukraine and the conspiracy that Boris had uncovered.

Before I had time to answer, Arthur pushed through his security subordinates, came up to me and whispered in my ear.

"We have to be out of here in two minutes. One of my informers has advised that the general prosecutor's office has issued a warrant for your arrest and they are on the way here to apprehend you."

"Okay, get the vehicles ready. Sveta... please, tell the guys from Huberman that I'll get back in touch with them sometime soon, something urgent just came up. They'll understand. Here, Arthur, please help me revive Boris, he'll be coming with us."

Shit, we needed to hurry. Arthur's mobile rang, he listened for a second and hung up.

"Too late, they are here already."

"Fuck."

Arthur answered another call from downstairs.

"It's the junior prosecutor with a warrant, backed up by a bus full of Berkut special police in full gear. They are here to arrest you, Misha. We must go. Now!"

Arthur ordered two of his men to carry Boris, and we hurried out to the elevators.

"Fuck, they are both coming up," Arthur sneered. He grabbed an Uzi from one of the guys holding up Boris and sprayed both elevators' doors. The fire alarm went off, but the lifts kept moving.

"The roof. Go!" Arthur shouted.

We ran to the stairwell and sprinted to the roof. As we entered the roof area, the sounds from below told us that our pursuers had arrived at the office floor. They wouldn't take long to realise we had fled upwards. Arthur jammed the roof door shut and we ran to the chopper. The pilot wasn't expecting us, and looked on, dumbfounded.

"Start the engines, you stupid fuck!" Arthur screamed menacingly, bringing the pilot round to his senses. He threw away his cigarette and jumped inside to start the rotor.

We had just hovered off the pad when the roof door exploded and armed men spilled out like cockroaches. One was holding a bazooka.

Arthur yelled: "Down!"And the pilot forced the stick forwards, sending the chopper into an immediate nosedive. The rocket hissed by through the place where we had been a split second before, and exploded on another office building a hundred metres away. We were considerably lower now, and some of the debris hit our chopper. Luckily the distance was sufficient, and it was only small rocks, and glass fragments, nothing big enough to harm the rotors. After stabilising the chopper, which shook a little as the explosive force rippled through us, the pilot took us on a slaloming course between the high rise buildings and didn't rise above the skyline until we exited out of the city centre. The police might also have choppers, so I wondered whether they had scrambled and were approaching to intercept us.

I looked at Arthur, who was calmness personified. His men were stationed at each door, scanning the horizon in each direction, alert and focussed. I was glad I had such professionals around me.

Romeo Drops a Bomb

Even if there was any airborne pursuit, luckily, we didn't encounter them. Arthur acted according to the protocol that he himself had written and adopted for exactly this kind of emergency occasions. We flew west, keeping low and almost skimming the tops of the forest beneath us. Our cell phones had been left in the office, so there was no-one to call. The monotonous drone of the rotors made talk almost impossible, so I settled back and tried to understand what had just happened. An arrest warrant is one thing - I'd had plenty of those issued against me in the past - but turning up to execute a warrant with the special police in tow, and an RPG as backup was more than a little excessive. I mulled over the event, and there was only one explanation I could come up with. Denis. The *whoop whoop* of the rotors had a hypnotic effect on me, I closed my eyes and thought about my next move.

'So, you are a big shot now and I'm the outcast,' I thought to myself.

No problem. Denis' reign wouldn't be long. Guaranteed by Vorotavich and Co. I opened my eyes and realised that Boris had finally come to his senses and was eyeing me angrily from the back of the chopper. He'd be alright, I thought. He volunteered to be punished, so he shouldn't have any complaints about my choice of reprimand. In hindsight, he should be happy to discover that some luck was still on his side.

We crossed the Ukrainian border into Polish airspace about a hundred kilometres north of Lviv, unnoticed neither by Ukrainian nor Polish anti-air defences. I'd been absorbing blow after blow and things weren't getting any better. I must counter attack, I realised, otherwise with the scale and multi-faceted nature of the attacks, I could be finished by the end of the year.

I made a mental list of things I had to do when we were safe. First off, I needed to contact David and get an update on the highway project in Belarus. Next, I had to know what those spies / real estate brokers at Huberman wanted.

While I was in the Cayman Islands, David had arranged a meeting for me with the head of the Ukrainian desk at Langley. I wasn't that stupid as to not inquire about David's mysterious connections, so, after my heavy but friendly interrogation, David reluctantly admitted that he had certain connections with one of the Israeli security agencies. He didn't mention who, specifically, but of course - it was Mossad.

When I wanted to visit New York as a regular tourist, they wouldn't let me in, but when the CIA intervened there wasn't a problem anymore. A bit hypocritical, I would say.

David and I had a long chat with Ken and Romeo - I'm pretty sure these weren't their real names - in one of the fabulous Greenwich Village restaurants in New York. They tried to impress me with their knowledge about my mishaps, the local intrigues in Kiev, and their general awareness of the situation there. They spoke perfect Russian and probably Ukrainian too, as they asked in which of the two languages I preferred to speak. Ken even half joked, half boasted that Google Translate referred to him when it didn't know a certain word in Ukrainian. But speaking the language is not enough; it has nothing to do with mentality. Maybe they were born in the USSR, but their mentality was too American. My impression was that they could analyse events and pinpoint tendencies, but they didn't really understand the motives and mentality that drives the Ukrainian politicians and establishment. They spoke of patriotism, where there was none; they mentioned benefits to the country, which didn't interest any politician. They were too distant, too theoretical to understand the real processes and to influence them. These were my conclusions and, if they had read my mind they wouldn't have been flattered. If Romeo was indeed heading the Ukrainian desk, then the Russians shouldn't be too concerned about any American influence on Ukraine.

However, these guys had some abilities, and Ukraine, as a buffer zone between the west and the Russian Bear, was one of their priorities. So, it was good to have a contact. But the most interesting part was concerning me personally.

As we were shaking hands to say goodbye, Ken told me one interesting detail that I didn't know before.

"You know that on the date you were shot, a person named Victor Glushakov visited Kiev and left the same day? It might have some meaning to you."

He grinned, waiving off my inquiry to tell me who this man was.

It didn't matter because a few hours after I gave the name to Arthur, I had quite a file on him. It transpired that Victor

Glushakov was an excellent sniper, often referred to as *The White Tiger*. He was the head of the special operations department - in other words, a hit squad - for the KGB during the period when the Puppet Master was its director. That was a strong indication of the sponsor and the executioner of my assassination attempt. I couldn't be certain that the Americans weren't just pointing me in his direction for their own selfish reasons, so investigating the possibility that this Victor was my would-be assassin was high on my to-do list.

In general, I'd agreed with Romeo and Ken to share any mutually beneficial info, as we'd all pleasantly admitted that our ultimate goals coincided on many levels, albeit for slightly different reasons. Mine was the desire for Ukraine to join the EU, as I believed this was what was best overall for my country, and theirs was Ukraine leaving the Russian zone of influence or at least achieving a substantial decrease in it.

After settling into a hotel in Katowice, which Arthur chose for me as a temporary Polish base instead of Warsaw, because the capital was rammed full with all kinds of special agents, I dialled the free international access number that Ken gave me in New York, and muted the TV on the wall in front of me. A pleasant female voice announced: "Huberman Real Estate, Angela speaking."

"Yeah, hello there. Someone called and suggested that you might have a condo I've been looking for in Manhattan? This is Michael Vorotavich."

I smiled at the James Bond spy talk. I imagined how the CIA switching software was categorising me as a caller and referring me to the necessary department.

"Wait on the line, please, Mr Vorotavich, let me check which realtor was looking for you."

In less than a minute Angela was back on the line, taking my contact details and promising that someone would get in touch with me soon. I got a call back in two hours, which relayed an offer to go to the American Embassy in Bratislava in two days time for a meeting with the cultural attaché to Slovakia. It sounded good to me. Bratislava was close enough. Why should I turn some culture down?

Okay, I had two days to stay holed up in Katowice, so I ordered Arthur to get busy with his phone and concentrate on the dodgy share sales to establish the ultimate beneficiaries of the seven companies sold for peanuts by Johnny.

***

As is customary, the American Embassy was the most guarded building in the entire country of Slovakia. Arthur arranged an escort of four jeeps to take me to Bratislava from Katowice with a tight circle of bodyguards around me until I entered the embassy's premises.

It probably wasn't the wisest move to go to a meeting in the embassy, as it was closely watched by Russians and other security forces, but I was in deep enough shit already and had to risk it.

The security proceedings were meticulous, but quick, and then a speechless lady, who stood statue-like, waiting for me to pass all the security checks, took me to the second floor and into an internal meeting room which was empty when I entered. Completely windowless, some kind of subtle metal frame surrounded its entire perimeter for anti-surveillance or listening purposes, I assumed. There were two replica paintings on the walls and a large table with eighteen chairs. Take the paintings and the chairs out, and the meeting room could easily pass for an interrogation facility. Its metal entrance door, grey walls and surveillance cameras hinted at its possible other uses. I was glad that for me, they'd chosen the more hospitable 'meeting' arrangement.

The door opened and Romeo, this time in his capacity of *cultural attaché* entered, in the company of another guy, introduced to me as John, who I guessed was probably a CIA field operative.

The same nameless and silent lady that met me downstairs, brought in a tray with a tea pot, water, glasses and some pastries. So much for American hospitality. I was curious whether our hostess / waitress was trained in honey trap skills, like killer blow jobs. Why didn't they send someone like her to seduce and recruit me? I would've been a more dedicated sympathiser if such was the case.

If Romeo came all the way from Virginia to meet me in Bratislava, the jetlag wasn't noticeable on him. He was radiant and alert.

"Michael, sir, I heard about all the dramas you've had to deal with lately, what with your brother's abduction and the raid on your office building in Kiev, and even some commercial bad luck."

Romeo's polite smile could've been interpreted as if he was happy with all these incidents. I hoped that he wasn't getting all this info from David on a daily report basis, I really wouldn't like that. His knowledge made me wonder whether he knew about the outcome of my visit to Kazakhstan, which again, I wanted to keep within my own close circle. For Romeo though I was eager to show that nothing much was going on.

"Yeah, you are well informed, I see, but that's nothing, dear friend Romeo. Unfortunately, that's all quite normal if you do business in Ukraine. Instead of respected competitors and colleagues, I'm surrounded by vicious serpents waiting for any sign of weakness to tear me apart. That's why I hope Ukraine will join the European Union one day. That should change the mentality, the attitude and introduce some decent business ethics."

Romeo was attentive, still politely smiling and nodding in agreement.

"And before I forget, thanks for the tip about the sniper. It put an interesting angle on the entire assassination attempt. It made me think that our so-called Russian brothers were somehow displeased with my activities."

Again Romeo nodded politely. The other guy sat upright and appeared tense, probably feeling much more at ease when wrestling with someone or breaking someone's neck. He studied me closely, probably in order to decide how best to neutralise me if such a need arose. I decided that the foreplay was over, so I asked why they had contacted me in the first place.

"But enough about my business. You wanted to see me, gentlemen?"

Romeo nodded again.

"Yeah, Michael, and it is because of the great peril looming in front of your country. We have reason to believe that there are strong forces opposing Ukraine's progress towards Europe, which is considered as a collision course with Russia."

"Really? So what is new about that?"

"We are certain now, more than we were before, that Ukraine might not sign an association agreement with the EU, as has been expected. Although you are experiencing some difficult times at the moment, we think that if you truly seek a European future for Ukraine, you'd better start applying all your influence, efforts, parliamentary mechanisms, your pro-European fund's campaigns and anything else to convince the leadership that Europe is the right option and not the Asian pact with Russia.

The smile vanished from Romeo's lips.

"If Ukraine fails to sign the association agreement, the knock on scenarios are very bad. I have some facts, all corroborated by solid intelligence, but I'm not at liberty to share them with you at the moment. And anyway: it's a bit premature to explore options that perhaps can be avoided if Ukraine does adhere to its solemnly declared European course."

These guys were worried. I could see that. The Puppet Master was outplaying them.

"Some scary news, I daresay," I replied, trying to keep an air of calm when inside was only turmoil. I was surprised at Romeo's statement, as I thought the association was inevitable as an official course of the current president.

"Of course, joining the EU is an idea I've championed for many years and to which I have dedicated my entire political career. I wouldn't want to see it failed. I'll do my best to prevent the gruesome scenarios that you say you can't tell me about."

That seemed to satisfy Romeo, who smiled and nodded. Their barely concealed panic had made it clear to me that I shouldn't put any efforts into saving the European integration process. If the CIA needed my help in that, it was probably a lost cause already.

In fact, I was going to do exactly the opposite of what they asked me - I'd order my businesses to stop any activity that supported association, cut funding to my "29-Ukraine" foundation, which promoted Ukraine as the 29th member of the EU, and any other support programs aimed at closer ties with Europe, and lay low until the dust settled. I couldn't risk confronting the Puppet Master yet and the understanding reached in Kazakhstan was that I refrain from any activity that could be seen as hostile to Russia.

Romeo looked at John, and both seemed satisfied that they had achieved their purpose in the meeting, Romeo closed the manila folder in front of him.

"Thank you, Michael, we'll be in touch," Romeo said as he stood and extended his hand.

"No problem."

"Oh, and one last thing...you shouldn't underestimate Chechen involvement in your current commercial affairs, Michael."

Wow, that was out of the blue, he did the same as the first meeting. Fucking CIA tactics, charming you, agreeing with you, then POW! Throw you off balance. I didn't allow myself to show any emotion, but already my mind was spinning. Denis and John weren't exactly Chechens, so what the fuck was Romeo hinting at?

The Handsome Trio

When we returned to Katowice, Arthur left me with six bodyguards, stationed on different levels of the hotel and another three near the door of my suite. He reappeared a couple of hours later with some charts and printed documents and spread them out before me. Arthur had all the names of the companies involved in the sale of my Neplokho shares, along with most of their beneficial owners. It was remarkable, taking into account what a short amount of time he'd had to procure them and the plethora of different offshore jurisdictions involved.

I studied the complicated financial sheets and a very interesting picture began to form before me.

"Hmm... insurance company through two corporate buffers stayed with Johnny. Understandable. Two more companies integrated into Denis's conglomerate; their new corporate subordination not even hidden. My fourth company's ownership leads somewhere to the vicinity of the Chief Prosecutor - Vladimir Pisotskikh, a prominent member of the Family. The fifth went to Gregoriy Vandalov - another notorious Family member, known for his connections with gangsters and the transplant black market."

I talked aloud, but to no one in particular.

"These final two. No leads yet?"

"Give it time," Arthur answered. "I am waiting for a couple of people to get back to me."

"Check whether a Chechen or two may be involved."

"Chechen?"

"Yes...like Mr Sanayev, here," I said, pointing at the remaining question marks on the chart. "His name may well be concealed behind the corporate veil of the same BVI company which purchased the shares in the remaining two companies."

"I see, yes," Arthur murmured, squinting at the documents. "You think Chechen?"

"Maybe. You see *Groze Fidelity Ltd.*' could be a play on Grozniy, the capital of the Chechnya autonomy?"

Arthur thought for a moment, then conceded.

"True. Chechnya has not been part of my direction of investigations so far. You could be right, Misha. I'll look into it."

"The way I see it, Denis kept Ukraine Metallum's shares for himself, which had a majority stake in the Ukrainian-Chechen Joint Venture, so I am sure that he must have found some way to appease the Chechens so they won't demand to reinstate their original share that I diluted a few years ago."

I looked up at Arthur, but met a blank face. Arthur had many great assets, but the intricacies of corporate business was not one of them.

"The 2-2-2-1 layout makes perfect sense to me, now. What a fair guy this Denis is! He equally distributed my property to secure himself and to raise his status with the Family and at the same time kept the most lucrative of my businesses – energy and steel production at his own possession. He gave one to Johnny for his treachery, two to the Family, who are now his *krysha*, two to his new Chechen partners and accomplices and kept two for himself. Even the communists wouldn't have been able to find a more just solution. Now we know who was behind the raid on the Odessa steel subsidiary and all the rest."

"Motherfucker. Maybe we just eradicate them all from the face of the earth." Arthur spat in disgust.

"No. As tempting as that sounds, that won't reinstate my rights over the assets."

***

Krysha - political back-up and protection - was more important than its protégée, so I sent Boris back to Ukraine, after Arthur made sure that there weren't any warrants against him. The purpose of the trip was to meet the general prosecutor - the official job of Vladimir Pisotskikh, who had profited from Denis' recent generosity. As with almost any Ukrainian bureaucrat, the official position just wasn't interesting and rewarding enough for Vladimir, that's why he combined it with the job of the prime raider of Ukraine, abusing his powers as the general prosecutor to strip others of their property and businesses for his own benefit and that of the Family. I needed to try to alleviate Denis's influence and to present my side of the story. I was sure that the Family didn't give a shit about either Denis or me, and supported Denis just because he offered something of interest to them. This something was my TV channel no less, that they needed for the upcoming elections. I instructed Boris not to demand its return for the time being, but to draw their attention to the fact that it was mine and if anyone wanted it, I would appreciate an appropriate payment. I couldn't openly demand a payment from them, but I could raise the issue.

"Be adamant, man," I instructed Boris, "But don't piss them off so much that you evoke some violent response. With your skills in this gangster palaver, I'm sure you will know how best to present it."

All was good with Boris again. We'd downed two bottles of Polish potato vodka the previous evening and got things straight between us. We'd experienced too many setbacks lately and there were so few of us left, so everyone was a little edgy, but we needed to put aside our grudges and move on.

After Boris hit the road, I dialled Gregoriy Vandalov. I knew most of the sleazy characters that had some influence in Ukraine, and he wasn't an exception, as two years ago he bought from me a Meat Combine in South Ukraine, which I'd privatised through an auction. I hoped he hadn't used it to trade human limbs and organs somehow. I was about to hang up after hearing many long beeps, when he finally answered.

"Da?"

His hoarse and mean voice growled through the receiver. Someone who didn't know him, would disconnect immediately, understanding that the respondent was not the nicest guy to talk to.

"Grisha, *privet*." I replied, in my coarsest, most gangster-like voice. "It's Mikhail Vorotavich, remember me?"

There was a long silence, then another: "Da."

"Listen, we have a small issue that you might not even be aware of, which I want to discuss with you. How about you come to see me in Poland tomorrow?"

It was a bit rude to demand he came to me, but I wanted it that way to show that I was above him as the boss of myself, while he was a dependent of the Family's hierarchy.

I heard some growling on the other end. Not a *da* this time. He was contemplating how to react to my straightforward approach.

"What is that that you want, Misha?"

That wasn't a *nyet* either! The fish was on the hook, just like I'd hoped.

"Not for the telephone, brother." I didn't want to leave anything for his discretion, so I continued matter-of-factly. "Tomorrow my pilot will be waiting for you at Kiev International Airport at 10am, I'll text you his mobile number. You'll be here in an hour and a half and I'll return you the same day back to Kiev."

There was another growl, followed by a long awaited '*da*.'

Party for Two

I had time to think it out in advance. Not enough time had passed so *my* company hadn't become *his* yet on a subconscious level. Besides, you don't value that much something that you get for free. These were my basic assumptions on which I wanted to build sufficient leverage on Vandalov to sway the balance in my favour.

Such a rendezvous was the dream of every hotel owner. There were supposed to be just the two of us, but I booked the entire banquet hall and asked them to call in all the waitresses as if to cater for a full attendance. I asked Arthur to send the same four jeeps that escorted me to Bratislava to bring Grisha from the airport to the hotel as an impressive show that I was far from being down and out. It's never a waste to show-off a bit. He should feel respected, and he should feel my might at the same time too.

"Hey, Grisha," I exclaimed in my friendliest voice, embracing him warmly when he arrived at the hotel.

I led him along the line of waitresses waiting in attendance, probably baffled by this bizarre feast, to a huge table formed from six smaller ones and completely covered with the fanciest of cuisines that could be prepared on such short notice. For someone else it would be just a tribute and a sign of respect, but in Grisha's case, I was truly concerned whether there would be enough food for the fat bastard. The last time we had dined together, to celebrate the closing of the Meat Factory deal, the restaurant hosting us ran out of dishes trying to satisfy the 120 kilo bear of a man. I had a feeling that this time I had more than enough to satisfy his greed.

We took our places and a waitress offered us drinks. Grisha chose a single malt scotch, while I decided to continue with the vodka, bearing in mind that the hangover after the last session with Boris wasn't that bad. The sommelier filled our glasses and after a cheerful *na zdorovye,* the game was on. Black caviar was placed in front of us as a light accompaniment, and Grisha smacked his lips in appreciation. He washed down the caviar, wiped his mouth with a napkin, and eyed me suspiciously across the table.

"So, what is it, Misha? Have you invited me to an annual mafia assembly that I wasn't aware of?"

I regretted that Boris wasn't with me as he would probably have an anecdote or two suitable for this situation.

"Nah, it's just two of us, Grisha. I thought you might be a bit hungry after the journey." I laughed, he cackled; let's assume that we got off on the right foot.

The sommelier spotted immediately with his experienced eye what kind of clientele he was dealing with, so he stayed close and poured us the second and the third drink almost without interval in between, while we were steadily destroying plate after plate of appetisers.

I wasn't that hungry, but Grisha was rather passionate about the food on offer. Slowing down my consumption before the alcohol's influence became too noticeable, I decided to try my blitz on him and gestured to the sommelier in the pre-agreed manner to make sure no personnel approached us until I allowed, so as not to interfere or eavesdrop on our conversation.

"You know, Grisha, when I heard that my Carton Packaging plant in Ternopol had changed hands and you became the owner, my first thought was to whack you."

He almost choked on an olive and his bullish eyes were quickly turning red both from alcohol and rage. I didn't give a fuck, as delicacy wasn't a part of my plan for today. He had seen my security when he arrived at the airport, so he wouldn't attack me here.

"But then, I thought, that it couldn't be you, that this prick Denis, who's a walking corpse by the way and you should know that, probably sold you some story, otherwise you wouldn't have gone for it. I know you, Grisha, and I think that we have some mutual respect. As you can rely on me that I won't reverse the sale of shares in the Cypriot company holding the Meat Combine that I sold you two years ago, I can equally trust that you won't try to take something of mine without paying for it. That is fair to say, no?"

I planted the hint about the Meat factory to show all possible consequences if he didn't comply with the request that was about to follow. I downed another shot of vodka, pausing to let my words sink in, and continued.

"If you want the packaging plant, its price is fifty million bucks, minus the one million that you already paid for it. It's something that I've built from scratch, investing my own money, and not something that I bought from the state for one fifth of its real price. If not, I want you to cancel the deal and return the shares and I'll send back your million. Think about it. You don't want to have someone like me as your enemy and we don't have any bad blood between us. You are part of the Family and your wealth grows rapidly, as you have your share of the state budget. Use it for something constructive. I know and respect you and I don't want to engage into a hard battle with an opponent like you."

After provoking his rage, now I wanted to give him some flattery, but I wasn't finished yet.

"I'm not gonna fight the Family. Moreover, I think we have much more in common than you have with Denis and I'm sure you will realise that soon. He's a small fish that will soon become a dead fish. The Family will need much more of my media, electorate and foreign connections, something that I can provide, while Denis cannot. But I'm not advertising myself, maybe nothing is needed. I can stand for myself and I intend to protect my property with whatever it takes. I've survived more complicated times, you know my story. I'm sure, Grisha, that I'm not mistaken about you and we will hug each other like brothers when you depart, just as we did when you came."

That was it. I tried to gauge his initial reaction, but either my intuition was silent or Grisha was a good poker player. No emotions showed on his broad face, which shimmered with a mixture of grease and perspiration. I beckoned a waitress and asked her to fill our glasses, to clear the appetisers and to start serving the main course.

Grisha growled, so I was prepared to hear his decision. He should've contemplated the pro's and con's already, and he was autonomous enough to decide for himself without the Family's authorisation.

"You know, Misha, you are some slick motherfucker. Not just a cunning Jew." Grisha cackled again and I took it as a compliment. "When everybody's sure that you are dead, it appears that you are just having a nap and here you are reborn again like the Phoenix."

Grisha raised his glass for a toast and said *LeHaim* - the Jewish variant of na zdorovye. We downed another drink, but I couldn't relax yet. He had to say it clearly.

"So would you tell me, how this came about?" I enquired, greedy for any info that might help me in further confrontations.

"Sure, why not? I owe that fucker nothing. Denis told me that he had everything sorted with you and the plant was the Family's to take for a symbolic price, but unfortunately you were in coma and unable to finalise some details. It was that simple. Who would turn down such an opportunity?" Grisha cackled again.

"Anyhow the plant is yours and I'll instruct my lawyer to execute the deeds to restore your ownership."

He took out his mobile phone, probably hoping that I wouldn't insist on him doing it right there and then, but I smiled and sat back, gesturing for a top up to toast our agreement.

Grisha dialled his lawyer, the same one who dealt with the Meat Combine purchase and instructed him sternly.

"Get in touch with the lawyer of Mikhail Vorotavich. You know him. I want the deal on the purchase of shares in

Ternopol Packaging Plant to be reversed, the shares returned to the seller against one million dollars returned to me."

Grisha pocketed his phone, and I got up, rounded the table and embraced him.

"Hey, Grisha, you are some very dirty dealer, but I knew that there was a decent man hidden inside you." I exclaimed jokingly.

"Now, that was an insult!" He cackled again and we downed another drink. It was my sixth or seventh, so I was glad we had finished the business part of the lunch, because I was quickly slipping out of focus, while my fat friend seemed to endure it much more easily. The waitresses were circling around us like bees around a honey pot, arranging the provocative and aromatic dishes of the main courses. Perfect timing - I needed something to soak up the vodka.

The aroma escaping from the bread pot containing jurek, traditional polish soup, was just irresistible, so I eagerly moved the pot closer and started emptying the contents, spoon after spoon, until the soup level went lower and I could break off the edges of the bread-pot itself. Grisha was happy to stuff his fat face with all the meats provided, and that was fine by me. The feast lasted until the evening, and at some stage Grisha convinced two waitresses to join us at the table so I let the live band, that I had waiting handy, come out and do their thing. Grisha had a whale of a time, and when he grabbed a girl and started dancing, I was surprised at how well he moved for such a big guy. The icing on his cake - as I was told in confidence the next day by the chambermaid who I caught changing the bed sheets, was that Grisha shagged the waitress in my room before leaving for the airport.

I laid on the bed, tired, full and a bit merry, and smiled at how well my plan had played out. Before I conked out, Arthur called and told me that he had found Johnny. This day just got better and better!

Mongolian Joy

The next morning I woke with a fuzzy head and rubbed my temples to try to remember something important from the previous night. The headache was unbearable. How much did we drink yesterday? I downed two glasses of water and then I recalled: "*Johnny is found!*"

I called Arthur, talking with my eyes closed and my other hand alternating between rubbing my temples and the nape of my neck, as the only way to cope with the devastating hangover I was experiencing.

"He's in Mongolia, would you believe? Probably because it doesn't have many extradition treaties."

Arthur was as sharp as a razor.

I hung up after what was a very quick call, and ordered breakfast to be sent up to me. It helped a bit so I called Arthur back and told him to be ready to move on and vacate our Polish hotel since we wouldn't be coming back. I then called Masha, and suggested we meet up in London in a few days time. Things were developing too fast for her to be located as far away as the Cayman Islands, and besides that, Watford United's next home game was to be played the next week, and after our glorious Champions League victory, I wanted to be there to congratulate my team, and to lap up the adoration of the supporters. Before all that could happen, there was a little side trip to be made to see my long lost financial guru. The prospect amused me more than anything. When the fuck did Johnny grow such a huge set of balls?

Arthur showed me the video footage he'd been sent, once we were seated on the flight to Ulan Bator. Yeah, I recognised him, although he'd altered much of his appearance. The disguise of a beard and bushy moustache made him look like Karl Marx, but it was still my old friend Johnny. He thought that was enough, so he hadn't gone for cosmetic surgery to change his face and overall appearance.

I wanted to have my fun first. On the video he was disembarking from a large jeep, so I told Arthur that once we caught up with him, he should take a canister of gasoline, pour it on Johnny's car when he stopped for a red light, and light it. From Arthur's grin I understood that he liked the idea.

The seven hour flight dragged on, I was filled with nervous excitement for what was to come. Eventually the announcement that we were descending in preparation to land was made, and I smiled inwardly. I couldn't wait to see my old friend's face when I caught up with him. Soon enough after landing at Chinggis Khaan International Airport, we cleared customs and immigration and exited the surprisingly modern terminal. We drove to where Johnny was supposed to be lying low; Arthur and I were in one car, while Arthur's men waited in two others. We all sat there for a couple of hours in freezing conditions until I was on the verge of giving up for the night. Eventually though, Johnny's jeep finally appeared from the hotel's underground parking garage. Gotcha.

We sat on his tail, forming a chain with me and Arthur driving in the last car. At the first relatively empty big junction, Arthur's men blocked Johnny's car from the front and sides, jumped out from their cars with open canisters in their hands, emptied the contents all over Johnny's jeep and threw a cigarette butt at the car, all in a matter of seconds.

The flames shot up instantaneously, engulfing the whole vehicle. Both cars then manoeuvred around and rammed the front doors of Johnny's jeep, jamming them shut. Too bad the windows were tinted; I wanted to see what was happening inside.

Time was running out for Johnny, and the jeep must have been about to explode, when Johnny suddenly fell out of the back seat onto the road with his bad wig smoking and his face as black as coal. He laid there, coughing and spluttering, wiping his eyes and spitting. Maybe he could use my helping hand.

Arthur pulled up slowly alongside the prostrate, breathless body. He jumped out, grabbed Johnny and hurled him into the back seat of our SUV. The stench of burning plastic, gasoline and human flesh immediately hit my nostrils. I turned around and studied closely his terrified face, greeting him with my most sincere smile.

"Hello, Johnny. Long time no see. How did you like my new joke?"

* * *

We left Ulan Bator as soon as we could. Our display was a rather crass one, and had probably stirred up quite an interest from all the security forces in that remote country. But before they even started an investigation we were already beyond Mongolian boundaries with Johnny happily snoring away behind us, courtesy of Arthur's little injection.

Unfortunately, I didn't have my own Guantanamo Bay for prisoners like Johnny, so I had to improvise. I wanted to blend in and not attract too much attention, so I instructed the pilot to get landing permission at Nice Côte d'Azur Airport, the nearest place to Monaco, where my yacht was anchored. I told him to send instructions to have the chopper from my yacht pick us up upon landing.

Johnny was the worst possible traitor, a real Brutus. Worse than Vova, whom I executed personally for his betrayal many years ago. Johnny, as opposed to Vova, was a member of my inner circle, but I had some pity for the poor fool. He had been deceived and used by Ukrainian scammers and then thrown out like an old prostitute. He was just a naive fool who thought too much of himself. With all these thoughts, don't get me wrong, a pardon wasn't an option. That would be a bad message to send out. But there was no hurry, as I still had my uses for Johnny.

***

We sailed into the open sea, away from French territorial waters, enjoying the still calm October day. Autumn was on the way as the breeze was strong and chilly, despite the shining sun and cloudless sky.

I don't like to interfere with the work of the professionals, but I asked Arthur not to be too hard on Johnny, as I wanted to talk to him after I had leafed through the affidavits, instruments of transfer, forms to return the stake in my insurance company to me, the conveyance deeds on Johnny's properties that I had decided to expropriate as a punishment, applications to the Police and State prosecutor's office describing the extortion and blackmail that he was exposed to, with all the names, details and other stuff. Everything was in order, already signed off by Johnny, admitting his guilt and criminal involvement.

Johnny sat opposite me in my yacht's saloon. He was tied to a chair with a gag in his mouth, but his bulging eyes were screaming nonetheless. I sat in front of him, chomping away loudly on fried shrimps - one of the specialities of my yacht's cook, and a personal favourite of mine. For Johnny it was the torment of Tantalus, as he couldn't take a bite, but that was the least cruel torture facing him at that moment.

I mostly ignored him, concentrating fully on my snack. I threw an occasional gaze his way as I was still undecided about what to do with him. Arthur had been a little overzealous with him, judging by the many bruises and blood stains on his face and clothing.

The entire story of betrayal had already been beaten out of Johnny by Arthur and it was just as obvious as I'd already imagined. No fucking novelty, all too banal. Denis courted and hung out with Johnny for a long time, acting like a normal drinking buddy. It was all good and wouldn't have raised any suspicions as everyone knew that Denis was considered my friend, and whether that was entirely accurate or not, that was how our relationship would be perceived from the outside. David and Boris knew that Denis was a snake, and naive American Johnny probably didn't. Once I was shot, Denis initiated a gambit that he had probably fostered for quite some time.

At their occasional meetings, Denis, who probably found Johnny's Achilles' heel in his wounded pride, often complained to Johnny about what a selfish and short-sighted boss I was when he had worked for me, how I didn't know how to pay esteem to my subordinates and so on. He preached that seeing my contemptuous attitude, Denis had left me and now he was a prosperous businessman, soon to surpass me in his personal wealth. Those words found fertile ground in Johnny's greedy mind, matching with what Johnny had felt for some time. Of course, all those small talks had just a single purpose. Subtly, Denis convinced Johnny, who he knew had access to some of my finances, to make his own investment decisions just to show me what a better manager he was.

After Johnny blew twenty million dollars of my funds on investments that Denis convinced him were secure and lucrative, Denis had a tight loop around Johnny's neck threatening to turn Johnny in if he didn't do what Denis demanded. It wasn't a single episode but a series of events during which Denis threatened, manipulated, intimidated and coerced Johnny to transfer my assets according to Denis's instructions. After Denis squeezed everything from Johnny, he sent him packing.

That was my fault too. Johnny was too naive to believe crooks surrounding him, and I was naive to never doubt his position and his commitment to safekeeping my funds and valuables.

I finished the shrimp and threw the plate to one side. Enough procrastinating! A few more minutes spent on thoughts like those, and I would start to cry about little Johnny's mishaps instead of doing what was right. I stood and walked over to the bar, Johnny's bulging eyes following my every step. I poured a martini for myself and threw it back. Opening a small cabinet, I took out a 9mm automatic and checked it was loaded. I looked over at Johnny and saw a piss stain between his legs. *Blyad, you can't even die like a man,* I thought. I walked over and took the gag away from Johnny's lips, placed my gun to his temple and released the safety.

"Misha, Misha, Misha..." Johnny mumbled. "Pl, Pl, Pleeaase."

"Shut up, Johnny. Look at yourself. What were you thinking? An Ivy League champion, you are a miserable cunt nonetheless. The saying *book smart, street stupid* must have been coined for you. You are a zero as a businessman, worth nothing, blyad. You don't even know how to steal and hide properly after so many years that you've worked for me. Look at you, you piss your pants like a child. Denis stripped you of most of the assets that you've stolen from me. Don't you know that the smartest students always work as consultants for someone who has balls? To be someone in moneymaking, brains are usually a disadvantage. It's guts, luck and instincts that you need. Someone clever will usually refrain from taking risks, while a less bright person won't hesitate. In business, even if you evaluated something wrongly, you do whatever it takes to make it work. Many go bankrupt, but some succeed. You are not made from the same mould, imbecile."

I was getting angry with myself for this lecture. It was too late to teach Johnny anything. Just finish off the poor bastard and before that, give him an opportunity for a few last words.

"Do you have any last words?"

"Misha, Misha, Misha..." Johnny still had some hope. "You are not a brute like many think." Johnny's miraculous riddance of a stutter had me briefly startled. "You don't have to do it. I've got a family. What would you tell them?"

Damn. He was hitting a sensitive nerve. I needed to pull the trigger. Now. I took aim, contemplating where the blood would gush the least. I began to gently squeeze the trigger, when my phone rang. Seeing that it was David, I answered, annoyed by the distraction.

"You lucky fucker," I sneered at Johnny, whilst cupping the cell phone. I put it to my ear and spoke with my friend. "Is everything alright in Minsk, David?"

"Misha, I know that you've got Johnny. He deserves any punishment you choose, but I implore you to spare him. I've proposed to his sister, man. I can't live with her brother's execution, bro."

"What? Come again?"

I was so shocked that I almost dropped the gun. That was the most stupid request I'd ever heard from David.

"David, blyad, couldn't you have called fifteen minutes later? Damn you. You ruin my little chat with Johnny."

Inside, I felt some relief from finding an excuse to let Johnny live.

"I'll consider your request, Dave. Jessica should be a very good wife for you, because her brother's fate will depend on whether you want to be with her."

Johnny understood what was going on and couldn't conceal an expression of joy and relief spreading on his face. I couldn't resist the urge, so I punched him as hard as I could, knocking his bound body to the floor, where I added a couple of kicks for good measure. I thought about throwing him out of the boat in the hope that some sharks would want his rotten flesh, but I couldn't ignore David's request. Fuck!

I ended the call, and shouted for Arthur to join me. I didn't want to see this fucker any time soon. Still simmering, I told Arthur to keep him somewhere out of my sight. I felt frustrated that I hadn't found an outlet for my rage, and wasn't certain I could keep my promise to spare Johnny. No matter, I would save my anger for a more deserving character - Denis Filatov.

How Watford became the Story of the Day

I didn't have to arrange management meetings anymore, as ever since Watford started to play in the Champions' League, everybody showed up for the home games. Even my mutual fund manager came all the way over from Singapore on the official pretext of reporting to me in person on our achievements in the securities markets, but the report's date, and its peculiar coincidence with the game made me wonder.

Boris was himself again. As soon as he came from the airport, returning from Kiev, he elbowed his way through everyone and barged in tactlessly to tell me that we needed a few minutes in private. I pulled him to one side.

"How was the meeting with the General Prosecutor?"

"Put simply: forget about Denis. Denis is the Family and the Family is Denis. They are one now. I don't know how he managed to reach that level, but it's true. Pisotskikh told me that if anything happens to Denis, the president would view you as his personal enemy. I wasn't aware that Denis had such resources to become untouchable. Maybe someone intervened on his behalf." Boris spat aside in disdain, wanting to get square with Denis as much as I did.

"Shit, man. Too many untouchables around me now. I guess my assumption about the Family's indifference towards Denis was incorrect."

I had to think over this knowledge later when I had less distractions, so I could find a way to circumvent his protection. I switched to lighter issues.

"You will love this, Boris. Did you know that our friend David is getting married? And you know with whom?"

Boris didn't look surprised enough for me.

"You knew? You are still a traitor, blyad. How come I'm the last one to know anything? I was in coma only a few weeks. By the way, you, an old fart, might follow David's example. I have a good idea for you. You should check how's Denis's daughter is doing. She should be fourteen or fifteen now. A good match for a paedophile like you. You could save another poor soul from my rightful vengeance."

Boris didn't bite.

"Thanks, Misha. Some good advice, indeed. Let me finish though. That was just the bad news, but I've got some good news too. First, you will get the TV channel back after the elections. View it as your kind contribution to the president's election campaign. They won't even change our management, unless it does something hostile, they will just put in their own editor-in-chief for the time-being. And, if there would be any profits they won't withdraw them."

Boris appeared proud of his findings.

"These cunts are really charming and considerate, huh?"

I knew I didn't have a choice, but to put up with it. I had been shown my place in the local Ukrainian power struggle and it wasn't too high.

"Another thing," Boris continued, "They might cancel the warrant against you, if they can be sure that your other media is supportive at the right moment. And this moment may be soon."

"I hate vague obligations the most, when I don't know what I'm getting into."

It could be nothing and it could be something that I couldn't do. I wouldn't know until I was called to pay my due.

"Let me think about it."

David barged into the room, wet from the autumn London rain. He hugged me and then Boris, leaving some droplets to my annoyance on my white jacket.

"Misha, don't send me to Minsk again, man. That's not the place for a groom. All those chicks are just too bored, confined to the damp Belarusian forests." David complained, looking almost sincere.

"Listen, mate, I disliked this wedding idea the moment you told me about it. I know that you wanted a Jewish chick, but Johnny's sister? I don't know what you see in her. Besides, if you have problems with Minsk seductions, then jerk off! Weren't you the one complaining to me just recently about your growing mid-life crisis? I thought you were afraid that no chicks would want you anymore and other bullshit like that. I take it that Minsk reinstated your ego and confidence with the ladies. Have you done anything useful except for enjoying your hard-ons? At forty you probably complain about everything: no girls - not good, too many girls - also not good. Jerk off in the toilet then, what more can I offer?"

"You want to jerk me off in the toilet?"

Seeing the lack of a smile, David turned serious and filled me in on his news.

"Okay, I see you are not in the mood today. So...everything seems to be alright with the project, Misha, the designing stage for the first hundred kilometres is almost over. Soon you'll be required to advance the down-payment, and they expect you to put your money where your mouth is, although the actual works are unlikely to start this year, as winter is approaching rapidly. Everyone seems cooperative, but except for our man in Belarus, I didn't meet anyone high level this time, so their cooperation doesn't mean much."

"Listen, Dave, I might decide that you spend your honeymoon in Belarus, despite your pretend aversion. That would be a good exam of your loyalty towards your bride. There is no way I can pay the down-payment until I return most of my assets, so you need to speed up this winter approach somehow or convince the designers that there is no special hurry to finish the designs, but you must prevent in any way the issue of the down-payment popping up on the agenda for half a year minimum, maybe even longer."

I was really worried that I might not have sufficient funds for this now and afraid the Russians might steal the project before I started to get the payments back from the Belarusian government.

"And one other thing, what's going on with Johnny?"

"Back in America, early retirement with no plans to visit anywhere outside his country ever again."

"Good, make sure he keeps his mouth shut. Always. If I ever see that traitor again I don't think I could stop myself strangling him."

My mobile phone had been vibrating constantly for a few minutes, as it appeared that dozens of WhatsApp messages, hundreds of calls, texts and emails all arrived simultaneously. I didn't rush to answer, being sure that the onslaught was about the upcoming game. As soon as it became incessant I was unable to resist anymore, so I opened Masha's message first, which read: "Turn on BBC right now. Love."

Bewildered, I switched on the huge TV that occupied the entire wall opposite my desk, and saw my own picture staring at me from the screen. A sleek TV reporter with a cockney accent was in the middle of a report.

"... might just be another assassination attempt. The previous one took place just over a month ago in Kiev, Ukraine."

Ha, ha, they don't know about Chechens trying to get rid of me in Israel, I thought to myself automatically, pleased that this particular knowledge wasn't at the media's disposal.

Boris and David turned around to face the TV and fell silent; I was still with my mouth open, caught by surprise.

The scene moved to my stadium, where another guy was about to interview the chief of local police, still busy in the background with some commands to his subordinates. What the fuck was going on? I mean the game was due tomorrow, but what does it have to do with an assassination attempt?

Finally, a red info strip appeared at the bottom of the screen, summarising what was happening: "An explosive device was found in the president's lodge of Watford Stadium by stadium personnel. Watford's game tomorrow is now in doubt."

Here in England? Who the fuck would do something like that? I didn't have a chance to take my ideas further, as my assistant entered the room and announced that two Scotland Yard detectives were in the reception, and wanted to see me. Except she was wrong, they were not police.

How Literary Agents can use their Downtime

I asked David and Boris to leave the room and told my assistant to let the officers in, after offering them tea or whiskey or whatever was appropriate for the rainy weather outside.

"Mr Vorotavich...I'm Special Agent Milton Stewart," the black, bald-headed guy said as he entered. He walked towards me, offering his hand and filling my nostrils with the not-too-subtle smell of masculine aftershave. He resembled a midfielder at one of our rival clubs that we'd just played, but I couldn't put my finger on the name of the footballer.

Special Agent, eh? So MI5 is involved now.

"Agent Stewart," I said as we shook hands, missing out the *special* part as he didn't look anything special to me.

"Jason Brown," said the skinny white guy standing awkwardly alongside his partner.

"Welcome, Mr Brown."

I acknowledged the obviously junior sidekick with a purposely firm handshake that made him wince ever so slightly.

"Please, gentlemen, grab the chairs," I offered, gesturing with open palms for my guests to be seated at the two Victorian style arm chairs in front of my desk, where Boris and

David had been sitting just a few minutes before. The TV was still on and the Chief of Police was now on screen reading a statement out about what had happened. I wanted to watch the segment, but seeing as the police/agents/whatever were in front of me, I muted the sound and smiled at my guests.

"So, gentlemen, what can I do for you?" I asked, as if they were a couple of salesmen.

Brown placed a Dictaphone on my desk, pressed *record* and reclined in the armchair.

"Mr Vorotavich," Stewart began, "I don't know what details you are aware of already, but it appears that you are a very lucky man. One of your janitor's was cleaning underneath the furniture in your president's lodge when he discovered a sophisticated explosive device and called the local police."

It was Jimmy, I knew this as he was the only guy who cleaned the lodge. He struck me as a rather dour and unfriendly man, but he was now in line for a fat bonus in his next wage packet. Either that, or I would see if he wanted to work with Arthur as an explosives detection specialist. Milton asked me something that I missed, distracted by my own amusing thoughts.

"I said, it wasn't your device, Mr Vorotavich, was it?" Milton repeated.

"Huh? No, of course, not. Why would I want to plant explosives in my own lodge?"

"Yeah, we assumed that much, but had to ask formally. Well, do you have any suspects maybe? Business rivals, personal problems?"

Having about a dozen by my last estimate, I nonetheless shook my head negatively.

148

"Maybe your competitors? We heard that you were wounded recently in Kiev. A sniper, I believe. Could these events be connected in any way?

"I am not sure," I replied.

"And which authority is handling the investigation in Ukraine?" Milton pressed further.

"Well, the perpetrator wasn't found, so it's hard to judge, but I assume that there definitely might be a connection. As of who's running the probe in Kiev, I'm not sure who does what, although both police and SBU are probably involved. I will ask my people to be in touch with you shortly and give you all the necessary details. Did you have a chance to check the stadium for more devices?"

"Yes, the whole stadium has been swept, and nothing else was found." Mr. Brown eagerly joined the conversation at last, speaking confidently, probably as someone who participated personally in the search.

"Gentlemen, I found out what had happened just a few minutes before you came through my door. I really appreciate your swift action, but I'm afraid I can't be much help in all this, as I myself have no clue as to who the hell would attempt such an atrocity."

I preferred to act ignorant and clueless. I would conduct my own investigation and deal with those involved in my own way.

Brown continued: "The device was so powerful, it would have destroyed the support structures on that side of the stadium. The entire western tribune would have collapsed if it had gone off. We must assume that someone planned to activate it tomorrow, during the game."

"That is disturbing news," I conceded, shaking my head in a great show of cluelessness. "Please, find whoever's behind this terrible thing. Regretfully, I don't have much confidence in Ukrainian authorities to be able to solve the riddle, but I do count on British security's expertise."

It was Stewart's time to nod in acknowledgment of my flattery. I decided not to share with them my little misunderstandings with the Puppet Master, Denis and numerous others. If they were any good, they would soon discover those details themselves, and I didn't want to steer the investigation in any particular direction.

We were done rather quickly and the two visitors left, stating they would likely be back as and when they either had, or needed, any more information. I thanked them as sincerely as I could muster, and personally escorted them to the exit. I headed back to the office and immediately dialled my stadium manager to find out whether we could guarantee security for tomorrow's game, and how UEFA saw the situation. The final instruction was to pay Jimmy a ten grand bonus as thanks for his good work, if it was him indeed who had found the explosive device.

While I was still on the line, David and Boris re-entered the office for further instructions along with Arthur. I told Arthur to enhance all security measures immediately, check our car fleet every day for devices and to activate all appropriate protocols he had for such occasions. The assault on me had moved to the UK and that was a rather grave development. Seeing as the details were all over the news, the plotter would be aware that he had failed and might have something else planned for me.

***

My parting with the MI5 agents wasn't long, as by that evening they were knocking at my door again. At around 10pm the intercom buzzed to report that a Mr Stewart and a Mr Brown were at the gatehouse and wanted to see me.

"With or without a warrant?" I asked him jokingly.

"Huh?"

"Never mind, just let them in. I'll meet them in the main guest hall. Send someone to accompany the gentlemen to the house."

I didn't bother to change out of my pyjamas so my guests would feel uncomfortable with having disturbed me.

"Hey, guys, long time no see!"

I couldn't help being a bit sarcastic when my security guy brought the agents to the guest hall.

"Mr Vorotavich, we appreciate your humour, but I doubt your mood will be so positive after you hear the latest developments."

Milton's voice was cold and official.

"We have evidence that leads to Russian intelligence being involved in this episode. We also assume that you might know why they would want to be after you and you should tell us why you haven't shared this information with us."

Russian intelligence? I thought the deal I'd made with the Puppet Master negated that possibility. I allowed myself to appear confused, and even a bit flustered.

"This is some disturbing news, gentlemen." Coming under direct questions, I didn't have leeway to avoid this topic completely.

"I was told by my personal security that the Russians were displeased with my open and fervent advocacy of Ukraine's European orientation, which Russia views as hostile to its interests, but I was certain that their enmity dwindled as soon as I stopped financing my pro-European agenda recently. You seriously think Russian intelligence would dare to blow someone up on British soil?"

I played the naive simpleton as best I could.

Stewart frowned, Brown scowled, both showing that my pretend outrage was laughable and that they weren't satisfied with my answers.

"Mr Vorotavich, you should be more forthcoming with the information you might have. We don't care what conflicts you might've left behind in your homeland, but we don't want any of them spilling over into England. You should be much more cooperative, otherwise we might ask the visas and immigration department to look into the status of your permanent residence visa."

Play time was over, Stewart was applying direct threats to me.

"Easy, guys," I said softly, in an attempt to lower the tensions a little. "I'm the victim here and I'm the first one interested in finding out who did it. I can sincerely promise you that whatever information or even thoughts I might have, I'm going to share with you."

"Well I hope that's the case Mr Vorotavich, you wouldn't want to be seen as hindering our investigation in any way."

More veiled threats.

"Be assured, gentlemen, I am as anxious as you are to apprehend this terrorist. As I said before, if I discover anything that may help your investigation, I shall be in touch immediately."

The agents smiled, but I could tell they thought I was bullshitting them. I escorted them to the door, and one of my security men saw them to the street. The fuckers were trying to intimidate me, so they couldn't have done any research on me personally or they would have known they were wasting their time.

As it turned out, I didn't have to share anything. I entered my study and turned on the television, flicked to the news channel, muted the sound and started going through some paperwork. No longer than twenty minutes later, my eyes were drawn to a flashing screen. A newsflash was reporting that British security forces, after a short gun fight, had apprehended a renowned London literary agent who had emerged as the chief suspect in the planting of an explosive device at Watford United football stadium. The name was as yet undisclosed. A literary agent? What does that mean?

Worrying Times

"David, do you know what the fuck is a *literary agent*?" I asked.

"Eh, what? Misha, it's you?"

David's sleepy voice was muffled and distorted on the other end of the line.

"Yeah, it's me. Sorry, man. I'm asking about literary agents."

"You are writing a book? Are you fucking crazy?"

"What? No, of course not. Look, I just saw on the news that the British security forces caught some *literary agent* implicated in planting the explosive device at my stadium. You should watch the news, man."

"Yeah, sorry. A literary agent you say?"

"Yes."

"Okay, that is someone who helps authors find a publisher for their book. I cannot say exactly what they are needed for, but it seems like they perform the function of sifting through manuscripts for lazy or overwhelmed publishers. My sister - Daria - was looking for one to represent her for a romance book she wrote a while ago. I remember her saying that some of them are real snobby cunts, but it seems you need one of them to get published these days."

"Well, there will be one less cunt soon."

"I am sure. A pretty good cover though, if the story is true. People in the Art's business get to mingle with the top society people, the rich and the aristocracy."

"I see. Okay, thanks for that, you get back to your beauty sleep, I'll see you tomorrow."

"Laila Tov, Misha."

After some thought, the bizarre idea of being chased by a literary agent made some sense to me. The problem with being a spy is that it's always a secondary occupation. For pretence, one always must have a cover life to hide the true mission, and to make it look plausible they must invest a lot of effort in it. Most spies are businessmen or journalists, so why wouldn't Russia come up with the brilliant idea to have their spy work as a British literary agent? If the suspicion of Russian Intelligence involvement was correct, that was some extraordinary disguise.

***

Arthur barged into my study, just as I finished the telephone conversation with David. It looked like I was going to have another sleepless night.

"It's Helmut Carriger," Arthur said, anticipating my questions. "The reporters in this country can pry into privileged information better than any special agency. His car showed on the stadium's parking facility cameras three times during the last week. Too much for a Londoner, visiting a stadium in another town when there are no games. The police went to his place to sniff around, and he opened fire."

"Motherfucker."

"Now he's being interrogated. Misha, you should try to find out some information through the parliament members that get free tickets to the football from you. We should be privy to every bit of information he gives, not a watered down version the authorities will no doubt relay to you."

"I'll have a think about who is best to approach. Thanks Arthur, go get some rest. I suspect the next few days will be eventful."

"Good night, boss. If I hear anything during the night, you want me to wake you?"

"No, it can wait till morning."

Arthur left, and I googled this Carriger guy to see what the web could tell me about him. There were a few hits, and one was a literary agent indeed, who specialised in military memoirs. That's a good way to discover military secrets, I thought. Nice, literate guy, judging from his picture on the internet. Born in Liverpool. Native Brit, but with a German first name. Why would someone like him want to blow me up? Because Watford beat Liverpool 2-1 at Anfield? Or drew with Everton? Hardly.

There was something else and Arthur had sown a great idea to try to fish amongst the parliament members, especially since several of them would be in attendance at Watford United for the visit of Real Madrid.

Smoking Gun

The game with the Spanish Galactico's was to be the ultimate reflection of Watford's meteoric rise to Europe's top table. Just a few seasons before, a midweek game could have been a far from glamorous tie away at muddy Rochdale, and now we were among the elite. Once the authorities vouched for security, UEFA was appeased and the game was to take place as scheduled. This was the first Champion's League game ever hosted at Watford's ground, and the fans were ecstatic. And we were the early leaders of the group, no less, with three points brought home from Milan, while Real had drawn 2-2 in Moscow against Spartak. Of course, it was only after the first round of matches, but I saw it as a good pretext to rejoice.

We were going to play a defensive, counter-attacking game and look for our chances on the break. The manager shared with me our basic game plan, arguing that were not yet experienced enough in Champions League football to compete with Real in an open game.

I arrived at the ground a couple of hours before kickoff, intending to greet as many VIP guests as possible, on the off chance that a snippet of info or two might be thrown my way. I personally inspected the VIP facility to make sure we would be providing fabulous hospitality in keeping with the level of both our opponents and the guests who would be in attendance. The waitresses were smartly dressed; the trays were filled with appetisers and the bartenders were busy making sure everything was in order.

I wanted to make the first home European tie unforgettable for the regular fans too, so I ordered 70,000 Watford - Real scarves, one to be placed on each seat in the stadium. The hundred grand cash kickback that the manufacturer passed through Arthur gave me some pocket money for a couple of days.

I had a list of parliament members that would be attending and I invited a few belonging to the Intelligence and Security Committee, hoping for a more detailed heads up on developments than Stewart and Brown would be willing to share with me.

Everything appeared to be going smoothly, apart from having to send someone out for more limes and mint leaves. I'd have to pull the F&B head to one side tomorrow and tell him to make sure his staff kept on top of such things. Still - in the big picture - it was a minor oversight that would only become a problem if everyone suddenly developed a taste for mojito's rather than the usual champagne and expensive spirits.

My invited guests started filling the VIP area, and as I did the rounds, ensuring I personally greeted everyone, I spotted Lord Barrymore - a fifty something elegant aristocrat, displaying a noble pedigree with his every molecule, enter the room. He was someone I hoped would impart some extra information about the literary agent, so I made an instant beeline towards him.

"Ah, Lord Barrymore, I'm so pleased you accepted my invitation to such a glorious night of sporting entertainment. Which was almost spoiled, by the way." I gushed with just the right amount of respect for such a man.

"Wouldn't miss it for the world, old chap. I'm glad the game wasn't affected by your little incident. Most upsetting, I'm sure."

"Yes, we were a little worried, it is true, but your security services are extremely efficient. If only my own country had such good men in these positions."

A little flattery wouldn't do any harm.

"A man such as you must be privy to all the latest news. Do you think it was meant to be a terrorist act or was it something against me personally and I should lay low during the game, so nobody attempts to gun me down from a helicopter?"

"Oh no, no Al–Qaeda here. This Carriger guy has been talking and he claims to be a sleeper agent, recruited by the Russians years ago. He's not controlled by the embassy, but takes orders directly from Moscow from the president's security advisor. Apparently he was given a free hand with the operation, ordered just to avoid using polonium. Claims he was unaware of the bomb's power and thought it was designed to blow up your lodge only. He says he truly believes you are a very dangerous person, therefore he didn't have pangs of remorse about his involvement."

I was shocked to hear who Carriger's superior was. The president's security advisor was the one and only Mr Puppet Master. So, the deal with him was off. My skin tightened in a mixture of fear and joy at the prospect of butting heads with my foe once more. He'd targeted me numerous times already, and I'd done nothing but politely ask him to stop. Negotiation time was over - I was going to have to deal with the fucker once and for all.

I thanked Lord Barrymore for his openness, assuming a startled look to appear like the titbit of information he'd imparted was the most surprising, shocking news I could possibly hear.

"Thank you so much for forewarning me. I had no idea that the tracks lead so high. I don't even know how to cope with this news."

Lord Barrymore smiled and shook his head.

"I'm sure you will come up with something, Misha. I may be old, but I'm not a fool. You don't need to act around me."

I smiled back at the aristocrat. He was right, of course. He might be old, but he was as sharp as a tack and up to speed on a variety of security issues that concerned his country. Hell, he'd probably been briefed about me when I first sought residency!

"Apologies, your Excellency. Sometimes it is difficult to remove the mask."

"We're all friends here. No need to beat around the bush or flatter to deceive."

"I should know as much already," I agreed. "But tell me, what is the deal with this literary agent? He's really a professional spy or what?"

"Carriger? Yes, these Russians came up with a rather brilliant idea. It seems that many retired military men are so bored that they actually start to write books or think they have shocking enough stories to try to put them in print, and once they have a manuscript they naturally want it to be published.

The market is so overwhelmed that they implore anyone to represent them and give them some prospect of publishing their work. That's where this villain came in handy. He positioned himself as a specialist in military memoirs and thus much of the officers' manuscripts were routed to him. To be fair, he did help some of them to publish, and make some money, but his system was a little different from his peers."

Lord Barrymore - the patron of British intelligence seemed excited with the new technique they'd uncovered and after enjoying a gulp of orange juice, was ready to continue.

"As I said, he had a system. Whatever manuscript he received from a former military man, he answered that it was rather boring and banal and that he had seen dozens of very similar stories already, thus appraising the chances to publish as below zero. He implied that a second or third draft was necessary, and if the writer wanted to increase the chances of publishing, they really should add more daring or exciting incidents they could remember. He was especially diligent and delicate with retirees from sensitive positions that interested him the most, and he knew who did what, and served where, immediately, as he asked for a thorough background from all the aspiring authors. Desperate for the opportunity to share their manuscript with an audience, the authors' frequently neglected their self-censorship, if not to say, confidentiality obligations towards the army or agency with whom they had served. That's a very effective approach to collecting military secrets under the veil of a literary agent. As you can see, he wasn't worth much in the field, as his bombing attempt was handled rather sloppily. But in regards to intelligence procurement he was pristine, superb even, I would say."

***

The game was about to begin, so I accompanied Lord Barrymore to his VIP premium seats and returned to my lodge quickly to make a few calls before the referee's whistle.

I called Oleg and told him that the deal with his other recent *guest* was off. I knew he would be able to put two and two together and understand why.

I then dialled Arthur and said in his own brief Arthurian style: "It's him." I was sure that British agencies were listening to my calls much more attentively now than they ever did before, so I wouldn't mention names.

I wasn't a magician or a telepath, but from Arthur's silence on the other end I knew well enough that he'd got my drift.

From Geopolitical to Personal

I was a bit disappointed that the game ended as a 1-1 draw. Not because I thought that we were stronger than Real, but because we had defended well, nullifying their world class strikers, and created several decent goal scoring chances on the break. We lacked experience in the Champions league - that was obvious, but we were still top of the group, although Milan, who beat Spartak in the other group game, were only one point behind us.

After the agitation from the game died down, I assembled my managerial board together so we could all go over recent events, and hopefully agree on the best way to move forward.

The results of our brainstorming session were infuriating, but regretfully sounded right. The general consensus was that there was very little we could do against either the Puppet *monster*, as I'd started to call him lately, or against Denis Filatov.

The former was one of the most powerful men on the planet, more so acting on behalf of one of the most powerful empires, and Vorotavich versus Russia didn't sound like a winner to me. The latter was supposedly untouchable. He didn't have the kind of backing enjoyed by my archenemy though, so his status would soon be put to the test. Oh, I could touch him, there was no doubt about that, but I didn't want to turn the entire Ukrainian establishment against me. Ukraine was still my prime money-making source, so I would have to be careful about how I dealt with him.

Arthur had plenty of ideas, but they mostly involved nuclear submarines, a fighter jet squadron and at least one or two tank divisions. Good old Arthur - he sure loved to fight, but I pushed his suggestions to one side for now. Never say never, though, if the situation deteriorated any further it might be the best way of going out with a bang.

So it was decided by the cabinet, that since I'd suffered enough attempts on my worthless life recently, I should keep my head down in my London hideout with Masha and the kids, while David and Boris would work the things out on the ground. Arthur would stay by my side, hopefully helping me to come up with more realistic plans for my retaliation than the all-out war he pushed for at the meeting.

***

Everything went quiet over the following weeks. Maybe my enemies were busy formulating a new way to get to me, or maybe I had been pushed down the list of people they wanted dead. That was unlikely, men like the Puppet Master are like dogs with a bone. They would come at me again, that was certain.

I used this lull in activity mainly to regroup my business, although it was far from being straightforward. The recent asset stripping of Neplokho had taken away many of my cash generating assets and I had to find alternatives to finance my ever-growing debt servicing expenditure. It wouldn't be easy, but I had to keep the group ticking over until my stolen businesses were back under my wing.

Naturally, I used the downtime in London to make amends to my family for the recent troublesome events. Masha was used to the dramas and understood that bad things sometimes happened to people like me. She understood, but that didn't mean that she liked it. I went on a charm offensive with her and the children, who seemed to act as if nothing had happened at all. You've gotta love kids for the way they can focus on the good things in life and block out the bad.

And there was football, of course. Watford finished second in the group, having tailed off a little after an impressive start. But nonetheless we managed to collect ten points which were enough to take us through to the knock-out stages of the competition. We drew Bayern Munich, which was a tad unfortunate as Bayern had been in fantastic form all season. But we were not going to capitulate in front of the Germans, that was for sure.

I hoped that my life was entering a more relaxed period, but naturally, such hopes were premature. There was another uprising in Ukraine. When Ukraine dodged the opportunity to sign an association agreement with Europe, I wasn't at all surprised, but the aftermath was rather astonishing. I immediately recalled Romeo's sinister prognosis for Ukraine in case it cold-shouldered the European Union.

Ukraine erupted almost overnight. The same as ten years ago with the Orange Revolution, huge crowds gathered at Maidan - Kiev's central square - to protest against the snubbing of Europe in Moscow's favour. I wondered whether my old friend Romeo and his bunch had used social networking to add some fuel to the brewing public discontent as that was quite usual in these days of instant news. These social networks represented too good a tool for prompting the masses into action, so CIA involvement was highly likely.

Both Boris and David were on the ground and were very articulate in their regular telephone broadcasts from the Maidan protests, keeping me updated daily on developments. A couple of days in, I received an agitated call from Boris.

"Misha, you wouldn't believe it, but it seems all of our office staff have gone to those silly demonstrations. When did that help to change anything in this bloody country? I don't even have a fucking secretary to prepare me a fucking coffee, man."

This was a truly disastrous inconvenience for Boris, so I couldn't help being compassionate, but in a sarcastic way.

"Poor Boris, without coffee your productivity will dwindle considerably. How about *you* take your fat lazy ass off the chair, make some coffee and bring a thermos or two to those standing freezing in the street, protesting against the way that the things are done in our country?"

Boris snorted, I guess he didn't think of his lack of coffee as a minor thing.

When the demonstrations first began, I instructed my managers not to interfere or support, but on the other hand not to apply any sanctions to those who missed work because of their participation in the demonstrations. Now that things were turning nasty, I authorised them to extend our full support to those fighting the regime.

Frankly, I didn't hold out much hope that anything would come of the gatherings, but I felt their cause was just and they protested and fought for my frustration too. God knows, how much I wanted Ukraine to be with the European Union rather than with its backwards neighbour. And besides, in my mind, you don't conduct politics like you set up a card hustle - and believe me, I knew how to do both. The leader cannot tell his people for two years that the country is heading towards Europe and will definitely sign an association agreement, and then one week before it is officially scheduled to happen, undo everything and tell the people that basically Ukraine is not ready. Politicians often neglect their promises, but here it was done so blatantly that the common people just erupted. They were fed up with corruption, plundering of their property, and a police and security force that seemed to operate independently and without recourse for their often brutal actions. The dream was stolen, and the population were angry.

The more resolute the demonstrations became, the more enthusiastic I felt and the wider I opened my wallet. I regretted so much that I couldn't go to Ukraine without the fear of being arrested, as I was sure my support for the demonstrators was known, so the deal with the authorities that Boris had brokered for me would be void. I wanted the authorities out!

I seemed to spend hours each day on the telephone with my people in Kiev. At first I approved supplying food and medicines to the Maidan protestors, and as the uprising became violent, I approved the purchase of warm clothes and protective gear to be used in defence against the riot police.

I seriously considered sending Arthur to Kiev to head one of the Maidan self-defence *hundreds* and to strengthen the protestors with our professionals there, but Arthur was strongly opposed to my idea.

"Boss, don't get so excited. Last time you sent me away, you were shot in the head. I cannot trust your security to anyone else. Recent events show that you are not safe in London nor anywhere else."

He pissed me off with his over protectiveness, but he was probably right. Something was strange though about the entire thing. I had a feeling that it was just another card hustle, so I asked Boris to come over for a short consultation. Boris had a great instinct for these kinds of things.

To combine business with pleasure, I ordered for us a VIP room at one of the Russian clubs in London. Of course, such clubs in Ukraine were better than their English replica's as they offered a wider choice of pussy, but I hadn't had an opportunity to visit the originals lately, so I had to put up with the poor substitutes. Arthur and two of his men came along for protection. He positioned them outside our cabin and joined me and Boris for the meeting.

It was early for a night club, so the place was still functioning mostly as a restaurant. Peter - the bartender that I knew and who always greeted me enthusiastically each time I came by, in expectation of a generous tip, was dozy and so were the waitresses.

After initial pleasantries with Boris, I wanted to share some of my suspicions and observations as an outside spectator.

"Listen, old man. I'm watching closely the chain of events with this uprising and I can't help being puzzled with some very suspicious peculiarities. In a nut shell, each time when it seems that the protesters and the government find some kind of solution or the events seem to start dying down, an unpredicted and unexpected event occurs, which rekindles the fury and antagonism between the sides. It looks very much like there is someone else involved that wants to keep the flames high all the time."

Boris nodded as I spoke, seemingly agreeing with what I said.

"I'll give you few examples of what I've noticed. Check this out for instance - just a few hours after the president announced that no violence would be used against the protestors and when it looked like the whole thing was about to disperse on its own, a violent crackdown took place, during which unarmed youth were brutally beaten by Berkut, wearing full gear. Of course, the crackdown's result was exactly the opposite - scores of new protesters reappeared and occupied the square. That's for one."

I took another gulp of my drink, happy to share my observations with Boris and partially with Arthur, who was present but I wasn't sure how receptive he was to these things.

"Ukrainians were so proud that their uprisings didn't result in human loss and there was some implicit understanding between the sides that lethal violence is to be avoided, and then the authorities break things up at the most inappropriate moment. There are corpses now, real victims. And all these people disappearing mysteriously. What's that about? Why aren't even the relatively restrained demands of the protesters being heeded?"

Boris nodded as I spoke, giving the impression that he had also started to question the possibility of outside involvement.

"It is true, what you say. I have been surprised at how quickly violence can erupt when everyone says it is a nonviolent demonstration. Such actions surely profit someone, but I don't see how it profits either the people or the government."

It looked like some kind of plot to me, one whose script wasn't necessarily written by any of Ukraine's conflicting parties.

"I agree, Boris. No good will come from this - not in the long term, anyway. I don't know if, or to what degree, the Americans are involved in all this, but I bet that the Puppet Master is pulling many strings. What do you think, Boris? What's the consensus in the government and among the protesters?"

Overplaying the importance of his messenger role, Boris even puffed up a bit before explaining his vision and knowledge.

"You still have a sharp eye, Misha. Of course, the peculiarities that you've mentioned are no coincidence. There is a big game going on, involving much more than the visible conflicting sides. Think about it: Along with the unorganized protesters that came to the square of their own volition, there are quite a few organisations with tight hierarchy, supplies and funding, that the security agencies were previously inattentive to their existence, that now represent the backbone of the confrontation. Who are their masters or sponsors? That's on the part of the protesters. On the other part, meaning the side of the government, don't you think that disengagement from Europe was *bought* rather than anything else? There are publicised incentives, but the rumour is that the deal is much bigger than is known. I know for a fact that Russian instructors and operators are present on the ground and that political echelons are giving instructions to side with the Russians. In general it's being presumed that it's basically the confrontation between the States and Russia waged through their different Ukrainian proxies."

"Yeah, that's exactly what I'm thinking, man. I..."

Just as I started to comment on what Boris reported, our waitress came into the cabin with a trolley full of dishes that we'd ordered, along with some extra treats that weren't on the menu, as a courtesy to VIP guests. The vivid red colour of borscht with a white stain of sour cream hypnotised me. Now, I realised what I was nostalgic for in my British exile. I took one sip and decided that I should tell Masha to hire a Ukrainian cook to pamper us with Ukrainian dishes from time to time.

The borscht spell was broken by a quite comparable, even superior show - the waitress' prominent tits hanging just few centimetres from my nose, as she bent over to put another plate in front of me. They would be a good starter before something as heavy as borscht.

Forgetting about Ukraine for a moment, I had discovered something that overshadowed my geopolitical concerns.

"What's your name, cutie?" I asked, planning my own attack and evaluating the loot she had to offer.

"I'm Jane, Mr Vorotavich, or Yana, if you like the Russian version of my name better."

She smiled heartily and showed a small and sexy gap between her front teeth amplified by cute dimples.

"Call me, Michael, darling. No dish that you bring can be enjoyed in the company of three men without women. I should talk to your boss shortly so he will give you permission to join us for dinner. That is, if you want, of course."

I thought that this rather loose opening gambit would induce some feedback about her attitude to my courting.

"I'd love to, Michael."

Yana wasn't shy at all.

"Good. Would you ask him to stop by for a second and also bring us the best Champagne he has?"

I'd arranged our meeting at the nightclub because there would be the option of a little play time with the girls. The waitress option was much better than the lousy and overused strippers that I'd expected us to solicit afterwards.

Yana exited, and smiling Boris tried to put me back into focus.

"What was that you were saying about Ethiopia?"

"Ethiopia? Huh? Yeah. Ukraine. What *was* I saying? Ah, the most important thing! If everybody thinks that there are third party conductors behind the scenes then the most important question is what is the *goal* of those conductors? And we, as opposed to maybe some others, know the answer at least for one of the parties. The Puppet Master wants to disintegrate Ukraine, to cause it or parts of it to join Russia! Bearing that in mind, I bet that the conflict is not going to die down until his goal is achieved."

"What goals do the other side pursue, in your opinion?"

"I cannot know for sure, but they are obvious, I think. The Americans, I can't know the degree of their involvement, want to sever Ukraine from Russia and weaken their formidable opponent. Not for some reunion did they plan to dissolve the USSR some twenty something years ago. While the common people would support them in the usual hope for a better government, a better life and to let out their dissatisfaction with the ever-growing corruption, poverty, tyranny and whatever else they dislike in their country. I'm just afraid that many will be disappointed after a while even if they succeed and overthrow the current regime."

The whole picture was clear to me now, except for how exactly each party planned to achieve their aims. And I must admit I was with the people. I agreed with the popular demand for a complete dissolution, or *reload* as they called it, of the entire government.

Could I help my chosen side beyond the charity supplies that I'd organised? I was sure I could, but I had to think how.

***

Yana returned with a huge grin and a bottle of Champagne that the owner brought for us. She joined our little group in the cabin and helped us annihilate it. I asked for two strippers, so Boris and Arthur won't be too envious.

Beer and Champagne are usually not a great mix, but if you add shagging into the equation to balance out the side effects, then it should be alright.

I told Masha I'd be home early, so there was no reason to beat around the bush. I excused us and asked for a separate cabin, as I was sure many were still empty because of how early in the evening it still was.

Arthur's shadows followed us quietly and stood guard in front of the new cabin, while I disappeared inside with Yana, taking the risk that she was the Puppet Master's clandestine assassin, intent on killing me by lethal blow job or some other covert sexual technique.

She was all over me like a rash as soon as the door of the cabin closed, unzipping my fly and taking my cock deep in her mouth. I didn't oppose that, but I wouldn't be satisfied with just a blow job, so I got her perky tits naked and bit her firm nipples playfully, sucking them into my mouth. I pulled her panties off but left her skirt on. Fuck me, she was sopping wet. For a second there I thought she might be really attracted to me.

I put the rubber on, which I always had handy for such occasions and moved Yana from a blow job to a doggy position with her hands on the table. Anything else wouldn't be comfortable in the small cabin. We went at it like rabbits, coming together and causing two glasses to fall off the table and shatter. I withdrew and sat on the bench, sated and empty. I hadn't had such a good shag since the Uzbek girl in Thailand, I thought. Yana slipped her panties back on and poured herself a goblet from another bottle of Champagne.

"Misha," she said softly, "I want to remember our marvellous meeting, and nothing's better for this purpose than to have a small token, like a ring or a bracelet. I just saw something nice in Soho, which costs only a thousand pounds. I thought you might want to afford me that small souvenir."

You fucking whore! I thought, despite my smile. For a moment there she had me fooled that her lust was sincere, but it all came down to the same well known axiom: I was a rich daddy and she was a little slut, not minding to give me some pleasure for a handsome reward. But well played, I had to admit.

174

However, my face portrayed none of those thoughts as I merrily counted out twenty fifty pound notes and wished her all the best.

"Of course, Yanochka, here you go. I wish I could have something to remember you by too, but if I take your panties it would be fetishism, so I guess I will just stop by from time to time to refresh my memories, if you don't mind."

She didn't. I hoped that she wouldn't need something from me to remember each of our *marvellous meetings*, but I bet she would find another pretext to get some money out of me.

When she left, as an afterthought I thought that I would've bought her a present worth more than a grand when coming around next time. But maybe she was right rushing to capitalise immediately. What if I forgot about being grateful after a while?

My phone started vibrating, I looked at the screen and saw the message: 'The Tiger is in Kiev. Huberman.'

That's one for Arthur to deal with. He will be pleased, I am sure.

Manhunt

Arthur agreed with me that an opportunity to get our hands on the White Tiger was something we had to pursue. I wondered whether Arthur knew this assassin personally, but he said nothing, and his face did not hint otherwise. Even the enormous Russian Army couldn't have more than few hundred agents of that highest level, and Arthur was well connected with such people. I looked in Arthur's eyes trying to catch any movement there, but he had the same expressionless stern gaze as usual. Unfortunately, with White Tiger as an adversary I wouldn't necessarily bet on Arthur in a face-off. Arthur, resolute as always however, was probably beyond such deliberations. For him it was an opportunity to punish the man who shot his boss. He was more concerned about my security without him by my side for a few days, than about his task in Kiev.

"Misha, you stay put in the house while I'm in Kiev. Don't leave it for anything." Arthur ordered.

Yeah, right, I thought. But I didn't want him to worry about me, so I conceded: "Sure, Arthur, good luck, man. Come back alive with the scalp of this fucker."

The message was accurate. Through Arthur's connections with SBU, he reported that White Tiger was definitely in Kiev, and was rumoured to be on the roof of one of the tall buildings surrounding Maidan. I didn't need to be a genius to guess that he was there to shoot either protesters or police, or maybe both to pour some oil onto the fire. Arthur expected to be updated on the exact location very soon, and was busy assembling a squad of fifteen of his best men to take the White Tiger down. Within the hour, Arthur received the call he'd been waiting for, and together with his men, headed off for the showdown. Choosing the route carefully so as to avoid a confrontation with either of the rival parties in the vicinity of Maidan, they made their way separately to the building. It was the farthest building overlooking Maidan, so it was no wonder that only the best marksman could use it. For Arthur it was advantageous, as it was on the outskirts of the conflict rather than at its epicentre.

At 10am sharp the squad stormed the roof. Despite the protective gear, five or six were killed on the spot by a blast detonated as the roof door, probably booby-trapped, was prised open by Arthur's men. The blast was so powerful that seven people were blown off the roof with just two surviving, fortunately landing in a huge pile of snow that had been cleared from the roads and piled against the building.

The rest of the group was welcomed by machine gun fire from at least three or four sources according to Arthur. Still having an advantage in firepower but suffering heavy losses, Arthur managed to get hold of the roof just in time to see the last opponent, dressed in white camouflage gear, jumping several storeys into the deep snow below. Cursing his opponent, Arthur watched as the man shot the three men guarding the building below and got into a white BMW jeep.

As it sped off on the slippery road, Arthur and three of his men were already on the way down, while two men were left behind to try and identify those that they'd killed during the shootout on the roof and take care of their dead or wounded colleagues. Once outside, Arthur's group split into two cars and started the motorised pursuit.

One of the cars lost control as it sped around a corner, and crashed into a road-block placed by the protesters on Druzhby Narodov Avenue, leaving just Arthur and Zurab, one of the last Georgians working for me, on the Tiger's tail.

Arthur had always been a superb driver, and was soon behind the fleeing enemy. White Tiger was excellent too. Using a shotgun one-handed as he drove, were it not for the armoured windshield, both Zurab and Arthur would have had their faces blown off. The chase reached well beyond Kiev to the luxurious villa area of Koncha Zaspa on the Old Obukhov Highway, where Arthur finally managed to get alongside the BMW and push it off the road. The Jeep spun violently, careered through the drift at the roads edge, then hit something, lifted into the air and spun five or six times before landing on its roof. Arthur struggled to control his own vehicle, which also left the road at high speed and headed for a huge oak tree.

"Hold on!" Arthur screamed at Zurab, and he hit the gas pedal and tried to use the acceleration to power away from the tree.

Arthur's skilled manoeuvre saved them from a head on collision. The car steered slightly away, and managed to kill some speed by executing a power slide as the oak drew nearer. They crashed side on, sending them into a spin. Zurab, who was unbuckled because he'd been returning fire throughout the chase, was knocked unconscious, while Arthur, his left leg crushed by the car door sprang out of the car and ran limping toward the upturned BMW.

Arthur approached the smoking jeep cautiously, peering into its midst while keeping his peripheral vision alert for any sudden movements from either side.

Too late - a huge blow to his right temple knocked Arthur off his feet. Still conscious but heavily dazed, Arthur immediately rolled sideways as he landed, but again not fast enough - his opponent was on him, landing with all his weight on Arthur's stomach. Pinned with his back to the snow, Arthur managed to dodge a series of blows aimed at his head, and reached for the knife on his left thigh. He thrust the blade upwards, but before it pierced his assailant it was knocked out of hand by a slick preventative move by the White Tiger.

Arthur used this momentary weight shift to roll out from underneath his attacker. They stood facing each other and smiled.

"Slotski, you fucker. Still working with the Jew, I heard." The White Tiger spat the words contemptuously.

"Better a Jew than a Russian mongrel. You prefer to shoot from a distance, eh, Glushakov. Can you fight like a man?"

The two old warriors charged at the same time. Arthur managed to land two punches to his opponents jaw, but the White Tiger stepped backwards and kicked Arthur hard in his already damaged leg. Arthur fought off the searing pain and went for Glushakov again, this time trying for his throat.

"I'll kill you with my bare hands," Arthur sneered as he landed on top of the White Tiger and started squeezing his neck with all his strength. The White Tiger's eyes bulged, and started to glaze, but in a final effort, he managed to buck Arthur from his stomach, and with Arthur still squeezing with all his might, Glushakov aimed a series of kicks with his heel at Arthurs injured leg. The pain was too much, and Arthur's grip loosened enough for the White Tiger to struggle free. Glushakov decided to run rather than continue in the hand-to-hand fighting, where Arthur definitely had the upper hand.

"You fucking coward," Arthur screamed at the fleeing figure, realising that his prey was slipping away. "There is nowhere you can hide from me. I'll skin you alive and leave you for the wolves, you piece of shit."

The White Tiger stopped and turned.

"Fuck you, Slotski. Remember to sleep with one eye open. I'll..."

The White Tiger stopped mid-sentence. He looked down at the hilt of the heavy paratrooper's knife that was embedded in his throat, his eyes panned slowly to his left and narrowed in anger. He fell to his knees, then face first into the snow. Zurab walked over and checked the body, removed the knife and wiped it on the White Tiger's white jacket, leaving a vivid red stripe of blood on it, then hurried over to Arthur and helped him get to his feet. Georgians were extremely proficient with knives and Zurab had come around just in time to finish the White Tiger.

"About fucking time," Arthur said. "Get his scalp, I want to present it to Misha when I return to London."

White Tiger and his crew had been wiped out. One of my enemies was gone, more would surely follow. Three days later, Arthur limped into the office of my London residence and presented me with a small box containing the White Tiger's scalp, taking my order literally. He never did tell me whether he knew the man or not.

My enforced period of lying low was nearing its end as Boris called a few days after and reported in shock that despite the recent understandings reached with the protesters, the country's leadership was running away in scores and most of the administrative buildings in Kiev were now abandoned and unguarded. The revolt had succeeded!

Why would they run, if the truce was agreed, signed and guaranteed by the West and the Russians? Well, probably because at least one of the parties didn't want the turmoil to end, especially in such a crushing defeat for the government.

We were nearing the finale. I didn't think the Americans had anything to do with the unexpected flight of the officials - that was surely the Puppet Master's doing, no doubt about that. Another and much more unexpected surprise was just around the corner.

Elusive Peninsula

I hosted a huge feast for the London Ukrainian Centre to celebrate the miraculous ousting of my political rivals. Things were looking up, but I knew our war was far from over. I was rubbing my hands in anticipation of getting squared with Denis Filatov, now that his krysha was on the run. I got an update from Huberman Real Estate that Crimean properties might change hands in the near future. I understood that they didn't mean real estate literally.

I didn't have time to do much with this tip off, as Crimea was snatched out of Ukraine in a precise premeditated operation. After barely exchanging a shot, the peninsula was swiftly annexed to the Russian empire, using the lame excuse of protecting the Russian speaking population from the savage Ukrainian nationalists.

This Puppet Master didn't waste time on fancy decorations. Everything was done crudely, brutally and instantaneously: the revolt in the Crimean parliament, the rigged referendum and Russian troops on the ground, wearing no insignia and pretending they were peaceful, Russian speaking aliens, all happened in a few days.

The interim government in Kiev that formed in the aftermath of the ousting of the entire Family, didn't have time to say *Jack Robinson* or *Dmitriy Medvedev* for that matter, as Russia's lasso was tightened around the Crimean neck.

As I expected, there was a personal touch too. The Puppet Master sent me his personal cordial regards in his own considerate way: my Crimean assets were among the first to be nationalised by the new Crimean authorities. It included everything: the sanatorium of Lugansk Steel that I'd renovated and turned into a luxurious sea club resort, Azov Oil's oil rigs close to the Crimean shore, my office building in Simferopol and a residential complex in Yalta. I'd lost another two hundred million dollars in just a few days.

And what a fool I was! I had an early warning of this potential grab, but wasn't swift enough to prepare for it or avert it. With such a tempo, instead of my aspiration to become the richest person on the planet, I would have to work hard not to turn into the poorest. Well, I shouldn't be complaining. I still had my yacht, a private jet and could afford the occasional shag with Yana.

The situation in Ukraine became very volatile. The entire existence of the country was in question, as the same encroachment as in Crimea was taking place in Southern and Eastern regions of Ukraine, where the majority of the population was Russian speaking.

The feeling of euphoria at displacing the tyrants was substituted immediately by fear, outrage and concern about Russian hostility. Even those who didn't like Russians that much had never expected that a brotherly nation would actually attack Ukraine. How wrong we all were!

The same experiences that I'd had in Israel, incessantly coming under attack from all directions, followed me to

Ukraine, as in just a few weeks the country was at war. I'd already survived quite a few crises and just when it looked like Ukraine was on the verge of the worst turmoil in its short independent history, I was actually considering how I could use the situation for my own benefit as well as helping the country out on the way, if possible.

Arthur has already received my orders to find Denis, who was now anything but untouchable. It appeared that the slick motherfucker, since he was not publicly associated with the previous regime, although enjoyed its full support and protection, was actually trying to establish connections with the winning party. What a snake! I had to act fast, otherwise he would find a way to carve for himself a safe haven.

I went through Arthur's plan for Denis and approved his idea. To my unprofessional eye, it was doable and that's why I authorized a go ahead.

Just as I was the King of Lugansk, Denis was similarly very strong in Poltava district, where his stronghold was located. If we were patient and willing to wait long enough, we would surely find a way to get rid of him whether with the help of a bullet, knife or bomb, but I wanted him alive and was ready to offer him the same trip on my yacht as Johnny had enjoyed just a few months ago.

I didn't have enough might to arrange a direct assault on his plant or residence - Arthur had been to his premises before and although we were sure that the security routines had been changed to neutralise Arthur's acquaintance with them, the numbers of the security personnel had probably been increased in anticipation of a possible assault on the building. We couldn't come up with the necessary might and fire power for a direct action, so we bet on guts, brains, distraction and deceit.

**

A forged letter from the Angolan Ministry of Agriculture reached Denis's table with an enquiry for the sale of a hundred trucks in civilian livery. My old friend Joao, who was now the deputy Minister of Defence in Angola agreed to verify its authenticity should any enquiries come from Denis' factory. In fact, it was a genuine letter, it just expressed a false intent. After a brief exchange of correspondence, it was agreed that an Angolan delegation would go to Kremenchuk for an inspection of the trucks that would require special adapting for the harsh African climate, as well as negotiations regarding the price and the terms of payment. One hundred trucks, each valued close to a hundred grand, is not a small transaction for any plant.

Joao, who I invited to my London office for Arthur's personal briefing, had agreed to perform the role of the deputy minister of agriculture as a personal but not a free favour for me. Deputy ministers rarely travel alone, so we had to form a team for him.

Arthur put forward his best operative to pretend to be a Russian - Portuguese interpreter, Joao, as a former special operations commander, volunteered one of his Angolan commandos to represent the ministry's financial and procurement department, while two more Ukrainians were to play the role of Angolan peers in the Ukrainian ministry of agriculture. Thus, we formed a team of five very deadly combatants for this mission. Denis's people were informed about the visit of two Angolans only, as the fax read: "accompanied by local personnel."

Having ordered tight surveillance over Denis's activities ever since the sniper added some lead to my brains, Arthur had recruited two workers at the truck factory to report any noticeable changes in security measures, along with any information about their bosses' schedule or movements they happened to hear about. The small envelopes these men had received for the past few months were about to pay off.

Certain our assault team would be searched, these men were tasked with smuggling the weapons into the plant. Arthur and I were both seated at my London office with an assortment of different communication devices spread across the desk in some order that only Arthur could discern. He was getting progress updates from someone on Skype, someone calling to his mobile phone, satellite phone and WhatsApp messages. Only postal pigeons or Harry Potter's owl were missing. For Arthur, occupied with the ongoing operation, I was just an irritating distraction. All communications with the team were made to sound neutral to counter the possibility of someone intercepting them. With the recent level of attacks against me, it was a sensible precaution. The weapons that had been stashed were called the *gear*, Denis was the *host*, the delegation were the *visitors* and so on. I nervously paced the office unable to relax until the operation was over. I memorised the timings and knew all too well it was still about forty minutes before the disguise would be waived and our team would embark on their real mission.

"Okay, the helicopter has arrived, they enter any minute," Arthur informed me. "They will probably go dark as soon as they pass security. Probably no mobile phones beyond that point for security reasons."

"Yeah, fuck."

"The pilot stays with the chopper. Any firefight or problem, we will hear from him first. Look, Misha, why don't you go downstairs and try and distract yourself. I'll call you when it is over."

He was right, my incessant pacing and anxiety were probably distracting him.

"You're right. I'm going for a walk in the park, call me immediately, okay?"

"Will do, boss."

The nearby park offered a much more spacious area for pacing back and forth and that's what I did, occasionally sitting down on the bench and surfing the Ukrainian news portals on my smart phone to see whether any news worth reporting was coming out of Poltava region, where Kremenchuk belonged. The sweat dripped from my forehead despite the early April chilly weather and my heartbeat was up to two hundred - or so it felt. I sat clutching my phone, praying for a successful operation. After what seemed like hours, the phone started vibrating.

"Yes, Arthur," I bellowed, startling a couple of old ladies walking their Pomeranians.

"Come," Arthur beckoned with no emotion in his voice.

The bastard.

I sprinted across the park, past my gatehouse and headed upstairs to my office, where Arthur waited for me, stony faced and expressionless.

"Well? What's the report?"

Arthur gestured at my chair and took a seat across the desk and started his dry and emotionless chronological report.

"At 15:02 the visitors were admitted to the truck plant. All five members were allowed in and greeted by a deputy manager of the truck factory, who volunteered to take them on a tour around the enterprise. Our assumption was that the false identities of the Ukrainian members of the delegation would allow us no more than sixty minutes before being compromised, so the plan was to act immediately once they got close to the management building. At 15:17 our insider handed the *gear* to Joao and my men, and the deputy director was knocked out, tied up and dropped at the warehouse area. Within seven minutes, using non-lethal neuroparalytic gas grenades, our team subdued the internal office security and started its search for Denis."

I couldn't stand it anymore, dying to know the result as all the events Arthur was mentioning took place over an hour ago, but Arthur ruthlessly continued his machine-like account of events.

"Denis jumped out of his office on the third floor in an attempt to escape but broke his leg and was cornered by our crew near his office building. Upon the team's approach he opened fire using a Smith & Wesson semi-automatic pistol. Joao, who was leading the group and not expecting Denis to be armed, was wounded by two bullets, but sustained no critical damage. Since you ordered for Denis to be captured alive, the men surrounded him and approached cautiously, taking fire until Denis ran out of bullets. Alexey, one of our men, neutralized Denis with a hefty punch to the jaw. As the factory workers started to gather, as well as external security, our team hijacked two new trucks parked on the demonstration ground nearby, and drove out through the fence and across the adjacent barley field towards the Kiev - Kharkov highway. These trucks are not bad actually, as they managed to pass through the thawing snow slush on the field without being stuck."

"Fuck, man - stop wandering off!"

"The last bit was improvised. An immediate retreat by helicopter was impossible because of the growing crowd. Getting across the whole compound to the chopper would have ended in a massive firefight, and maybe the mission would be unsuccessful. The chopper took off as soon as the trucks fled, and picked them up on the highway before a pursuit even began. Denis is already out of Ukraine and on the way to the French Riviera, where, if you so desire, we can meet him in approximately two hours."

Arthur grinned finally. The old goat had been playing with me, purposely dragging out the story and enjoying seeing me squirm. I let out a huge sigh and slumped back in my chair as the adrenaline pumped up by my nervousness finally dumped.

"You motherfucker, Arthur." I said, my grin now mirroring his own. "We did it, man. Great planning."

I shook off my brief stupor, jumped to my feet, and rounded the table to hug Arthur.

"Blyad, suka, finally!" I shouted.

Even if Watford won the Champions League, I wouldn't be as elated as I was now.

"Arthur, get together whatever you think we might need, call the pilot and tell him to get ready, we're heading to the yacht."

Arthur nodded, a brief smile flashed across his face in anticipation of finally dealing with the traitor, Denis Filatov.

Carnival Cruise

I expected to find Denis in the same terrified state as Johnny when he was brought to my yacht, but that wasn't the case. I entered the cabin and was surprised to see him self-confident and maybe even upbeat. Didn't the stupid fucker realise he wouldn't be alive much longer? Nevertheless, I smiled warmly and said: "Hello, old friend. It's been a while."

Denis sat up straight, and I could tell he was hiding the agony of his broken leg, which had been roughly bandaged by Arthur's men. Other than the odd grimace, and the swelling on the side of his face where he'd been knocked out, he appeared to be in fairly good shape.

"Ah, Misha. I've been expecting you," he hissed angrily. "Do it, coward. Get it over with."

I smiled my friendliest grin and replied with: "Later, old friend, I just wanted to say hi before I attend to some other business. We shall catch up a little later. Don't go anywhere - I'll be back soon."

I insisted we go visit Joao first, for whom we'd organised a room at a secluded private hospital for his recovery. A generous donation ensured that any information that their latest patient was suffering from gunshot wounds wouldn't leak out.

Joao was high-spirited when we entered his private room, probably more from the morphine injections than anything else.

"Senhor Misha, Sir, it was such a lovely experience," he babbled. "We captured that bad white man. Sir, poor Master Jeego, I come to his memorial from time to time. He was a great warrior."

My old friend Joao still talked like a baby, referring to Gigo, my late friend and chief of security killed in Angola, as Master Jeego. Seeing that Joao was high and wouldn't stop talking any time soon, I quickly hugged him and thanked him for the brilliant operation. My non-verbal gratitude was already on its way to his off-shore bank account. Seeing that Joao was okay, I felt that I could turn to the main dish - my old friend, Denis.

The car ride back to the marina seemed to take forever. I was itching to get my hands on the bastard, and wondered if his bravado had waned since I saw him, as the anticipation of a world of pain started to sink in.

He was nothing of the sort - in fact this time he was angry and spitting venom as I entered the cabin.

"Fuck you, Misha, it was a terrible blunder on your part to kidnap me like this. You will regret it very soon. You don't even know..."

I stepped forward and punched him in the face as hard as I could. All the hatred that had accumulated for the past few months was channelled into one powerful straight right. He fell backwards and bounced back from the sofa cushions, blood dripping from his nose. He spat some blood, the look of hatred almost animal-like, and I punched him again and again and again until he went limp. I left him on the floor and went to clean myself up, realising that my fists were like sodden rags, full of Denis' blood. I passed a crew member who stood back with a startled look on seeing his blood-soaked boss, a murderous look on my face, stroll casually past him.

"Get a bucket of water and pour it over the man inside my cabin." I ordered the crewman. "Wake the fucker up - I haven't finished my chat yet."

The man nodded and hurried off to carry out my order.

"And tell the captain I want to head out in twenty minutes," I shouted after him.

When I'd bought the yacht, I'd hoped to enjoy relaxing cruises around the fabulous beaches and harbours of the Mediterranean, visiting Ibiza's night clubs when alone or secluded Sardinian family resorts when accompanied by Masha and the kids. Instead, the luxury vessel had somehow become my interrogation facility.

After fifteen minutes I was ready for round two. I changed my clothes and cleaned up, feeling a little ashamed that I had failed to control my temper, but not at all about beating Denis. He deserved more than that and my punching practice wasn't over yet.

Now I liked Denis's look much better. Some cuts on his face were still bleeding, his upper lip was swollen and his right eye was beginning to bulge grotesquely. I still didn't like his angry stare, so I punched him in the stomach, making him exhale sharply and start coughing. Satisfied that I'd relieved some of my grudge towards Denis, now I could chat a bit with my old buddy.

"Why, Denis, how can I regret such a brotherly meeting between us? Why didn't you defend or punch back, by the way? Ah, the ropes, I see now. I didn't notice them, man, sorry. Want some more punches or you want to talk a bit?" I was beginning to enjoy this.

Denis eyed me warily, the cockiness now receding rapidly. The engines fired up, and the yacht sat up in the water and began to move out of the marina and into open water.

"You feel that? Time for a little cruise, I am sure you will enjoy it."

It wasn't a direct threat, but the look on Denis' swollen face betrayed his mounting fear. The yacht lurched as we exited the calm waters of the harbour, rocking me on my feet.

"It's a little rough out there, don't you think? I would hate to be out there alone, no lifebelt or raft."

"Misha, if you think that my patrons were the Family and I have no krysha now they are gone, you are mistaken. I was forced *on* the Family by the Russians and I have very powerful backing in Moscow. I'm sure, that soon someone will ring you and you will need to beg for forgiveness."

"Really?" I punched him in the stomach again and kicked his broken leg. This time he shrieked and almost cried with pain.

"What is this? Some childish tiff? Are you gonna call for your father to protect you? It is you, who's mistaken, Deniska!" I referred to him diminutively, adding insult to injury. "The Russians don't have leverage on me anymore, as my Crimean assets are already taken by them. I don't give a fuck about them. They are my enemies with or without you. Don't count on them too much, my friend."

Denis still begged to be saved.

"Misha, you don't understand, my krysha is the security advisor of the Russian president and he's my father ...."

"What the fuck!"

Lately, life had been so full of surprises, but this one was truly shocking.

"The Puppet Master is your father? Fuck! This cunt just keeps turning up in my business. Your father didn't tell you, I guess, but I will. Your kind and protective father cruelly raped the mother of my wife, which by the sounds of it, is your little sister. Just as she's not proud of her father, I don't think she would be so proud of you, either."

Denis was quiet, trying to work out who was related to whom, and whether there was some way this information would save him.

"So you and me...we are brothers-in-law?" He finally said.

"In lawlessness. You are no family of mine, blyad," I spat angrily

I did the same as with Johnny - I walked to the bar, poured a martini and chugged it back, then opened the small cabinet to get my gun. Fuck...it wasn't there. I left the saloon and found Arthur resting in his quarters.

"It is time. Give me the gun you took from the saloon and hid." I ordered him.

Arthur unlocked and opened the drawer in his bedside table and I almost snatched it from his hand.

"I want to see," Arthur implored. "Let me be there."

I gripped the gun tightly and made sure the silencer was secured.

"Sure. Come say goodbye to our old friend."

Denis screamed when he saw me enter with the silenced gun in hand. After the setback with Johnny, I was determined that nothing would obstruct my righteous revenge. I shot Denis first between his wide-open eyes and then to the heart area of his prostrate body. I stood over the lifeless body, and I felt...nothing.

"Take care of this, Arthur, and throw the carpet overboard too," I ordered, and grabbed a bottle of Courvoisier, poured a full glass and downed it in one, my hands still trembling with fury and adrenaline.

"We are square, my friend," I thought, as Arthur wrapped the carpet around Denis' dead body.

Now that the regime had changed, I wasn't afraid of an unfair trial and I didn't need Denis alive. I would make sure the courts would return to me everything that the motherfucker had stolen from me. I decided not to tell Masha anything about Denis being her brother. She knew him and never liked him, sensing with her woman's intuition his rotten nature.

I went out to the deck together with Arthur to throw all the evidence over board. Standing at the rear of the yacht, struggling with the dead weight, I spotted a massive dark shape emerging from the sea some distance away. Arthur spotted it too and squinted into the distance, trying to work out what the hell it was.

"I think...Fuck! That's a sub!" Arthur shouted.

We stood there open-mouthed, still holding each end of the bag containing the carpet-wrapped body. And then we saw something moving rapidly towards us, leaving white water foam behind it.

"Torpedo!" Arthur shouted again. "Torpedo! Run!" Arthur yelled for the third time, now even louder so the crew would hear him. The captain or the helmsman noticed it too and somebody announced over the loudspeaker:*"Torpedo! Abandon the ship immediately!"*

Arthur grabbed me and pushed me towards one of the jet ski's that were fastened to the rear deck where we had been disposing of Denis.

"Quick, we'll use this."

Arthur detached the jet ski, I had already fired it up and sped away with Arthur sitting behind me, pulling back on the throttle as soon as it touched the water. I looked back and saw people jumping into the sea, desperate to escape. Just as the chopper started to rise above the deck, the ship exploded from a direct impact of the torpedo, the blast consuming the chopper, which was still too close to the yacht. The chopper went down, the yacht was scattered with debris, and the fireball grew and then split into blazing pockets of fire that covered the whole area where my beautiful boat had once been. The shock wave reached us, and pushed us forward, but luckily we were already far enough away that we just kept on going.

Wow, they didn't even bother trying to free Denis. How fatherly. I was sure they knew he was on board. *Or did they?* I thought to myself, still shocked about what had just happened.

"Arthur, I'm turning back to see whether we can pick someone up," I yelled behind me, hoping he would hear.

"No, you go straight ahead!" Arthur commanded. "Russians are after you. The sub will send a boat out there. I'll alert the coast guards that the ship exploded so they'll send a rescue team to search for survivors."

Fortunately, the jet ski had enough fuel to reach the coast. I looked back as we neared the shore and the sub had already disappeared back into the depths of the Mediterranean Sea. How it had found us so soon was unbelievable. The Russians must've kept one patrolling the French and Italian ports on a constant basis to have demonstrated such a speedy response to my arrival. And how did they know I was onboard? My recent upswing in fortunes had made me complacent. The Russians probably had someone watching my house, my jet and my yacht all along. Crafty fuckers.

The rescue team picked up seven crew still alive, another jet ski reached the coast with two more. Five were missing and two were dead when they were pulled from the water.

Luckily, Denis's corpse wasn't found. The bag with heavy ballast, carpet and corpse was already prepared by Arthur so it probably sank quickly when the yacht exploded. Arthur reported to the coast guards, who stood open-mouthed in disbelief when he stated that the yacht had been hit by a torpedo.

We understood immediately that the French had found evidence confirming the existence of both the torpedo and the Russian sub, when my captain was urgently summoned to the prosecutor's office a few days after the incident. He was practically forced to sign a non-disclosure notice because of French concern's for national security. The investigation was to be left with an open status, meaning the details would never be reported to the public. With such a status, I had a problem with claiming the insurance for my yacht. God damn it!

Denis was right, the Russians did react fast to his disappearance, but they never bothered to come to his rescue. Having both him and me dead was just as good an option for them. This Puppet Master was just like Stalin who supposedly refused to trade his own son, who had been captured by the Nazi's, for Field Marshal Paulus, who had surrendered near Stalingrad. Legend has it that Stalin declared that he wouldn't trade a lowly soldier for a field marshal.

I asked Arthur to identify one of the corpses pulled from the sea as Mikhail Vorotavich or to just report me missing. He chose the latter option, to give an opportunity to mourn for those who were really killed, and allow for a proper burial for the recovered bodies. Meanwhile, I used a payphone - a more discrete communication device, to call Masha, so she wouldn't be too worried when she heard that I was missing, presumed dead, on the news.

I was probably on the top ten list of worst nemeses of the Russian empire, if they cared to send a sub after me. While *dead* or *missing*, I had to find a way to get rid of the Puppet Master, because next time they would use a ballistic missile on me, maybe even with a nuclear warhead. The Count of Monte Cristo had twenty years of imprisonment to plan his escape and revenge. I doubted that I had even twenty days.

The Battle for Lugansk

The explosion in the Mediterranean was the top news item along with the severe escalation in fighting between separatists and Ukrainian forces in the Donetsk and Lugansk regions. Somehow I felt that my series of miraculous escapes was exhausted and the next attempt would be fatal. I had to try to prevent it.

Masha waited for me at the airport. It was all too much for her. With tears in her eyes, she pleaded:

"Misha, we must do something so it will all stop. Give them all your money and companies, we can manage without them. Don't try to take on this evil Puppet Master. God, if such a thing exists, should punish him for all the atrocities he has committed. Otherwise, they will get you sooner or later and me and our children too."

I didn't have a clue how to soothe and placate her; moreover I felt the same about the peril looming over me and my family.

"I wish it was about the money, Masha, but I'm afraid that it's not what they are after. It's existential now. I won't let anything happen to the family, don't worry. They might dare doing *me* in, in London, but you and the kids are safe. They won't mess with secondary targets on foreign turf."

I hoped that my assumption was correct. I wanted Masha to believe in what I said, even if I wasn't so sure myself. She just kept crying and I hugged her, not knowing what else to say. Finally, I decided that I must give her something optimistic to dwell on, even if it was a lie.

"We have a plan to solve this deadly limbo. I hope we can realise it soon."

A white lie can be good psychotherapy sometimes.

***

I didn't plan to keep up the *missing presumed dead* line for too long, as I was sure that my survival would soon be discovered, since journalists had started their own investigations into what had happened barely a dozen kilometres from the French coast. I was sure that the world would be aghast once they had proof that it was a torpedo. And they would find out, I was certain, no matter how hard French authorities tried to conceal their own findings.

If I had heeded Masha's request, I could've tried to escape somewhere in the deepest Amazon jungle under a false identity for a while, but I didn't believe they wouldn't locate me even there. Stalin's assassins tracked down Trotsky, his former colleague, in Mexico, equipped with much less sophisticated tracking abilities and devices than existed today. In the modern era, it was too difficult to escape completely. No matter what I did, sooner or later they would track me down; I had no doubt about that. I was no Osama, able to lay low for years, and I didn't want that, especially now when Ukraine was suffering such terrible atrocities at the hands of their so-called brothers.

***

The Ukrainian people who swarmed Maidan, sacrificed their lives in order to oust the Family, and everything associated with their rule, in the desperate hope of changing the embedded corruption that affected every aspect of their lives and to bring new, clean politicians to power. Several months had passed but no sizeable change had occurred. If anything, the situation and ultimately the people's wellbeing became worse.

"We are at war!" The members of the new governing team were saying. "We will implement reforms only when the situation allows," was the gist of the rhetoric spouted by the new rulers.

And there was a war going on indeed, and the people grudgingly agreed to wait. I was certain that such tolerance wouldn't last long. If those who came to power in the wake of the uprising wouldn't deliver on their promises, their rule would be short-lived. The Ukrainians paid with their blood for the change and they wouldn't give up on it without another fight.

On a personal level I had to reassess my own conduct in the country. I didn't believe that generation-long roots of corruption could be severed in a few weeks, months or even years, but I did hope that we'd eventually have a cleaner country. There was a chance to change something and it shouldn't be blown. I had to have faith that it would happen, and began by cleaning up my own affairs. However, decency is only relevant to how it is measured - I was under no illusions that I was going to turn into a saint.

***

A message from Boris was waiting for me when I stepped into the office. What the fuck! The interim government had offered me the position of the Governor of Lugansk! Their reasoning was pretty sound - no one else in the district had more influence on the security forces, police, army veterans or the respect of the local people than me. I was seen as someone who could unite and lead the locals during the difficult times that lay ahead.

The separatists' troops, at first, were formed mostly from misled locals, turned into zombies by Russian propaganda, and subordinated to Russian intelligence military officers. They enjoyed regular Russian military supplies and helped Russian forces fight for Donetsk and Lugansk independence from Ukraine, or Russian dependence, depending on how you looked at it. They fought against Ukrainian army and pro-Ukrainian volunteer troops, some of which were financed by oligarchs. Small towns and districts changed hands frequently, conquered in turn by Russian, pro-Russian and pro-Ukrainian troops.

Each such region, being at odds with the central power in Kiev, needed the firm hand of someone with authority. To propose a governor's position to me was a brilliant idea, except I wasn't available, I was still 'missing' in the Mediterranean.

The overall idea was still a sound one though, so I *volunteered* Boris.

I called him and after dispelling his doubts that it was really me, I filled him in on the situation.

"Boris, I want you to take up the governor's position in Lugansk. Think about it, if anyone can help this region to stay with Ukraine it's probably only you or me. In fact, more you than me."

"I don't know...It's a lot of responsibility."

"Look, make Stepan - your friend and manager of the biggest factory in the district, your deputy and make our managers and trade union leaders responsible for the different needs of the region. We must cut the separatists from whatever scarce support they might have from local people, and with those guys in place, it can be done. We have enough men and support to organise adequate security forces to cooperate and help with troops sent from Kiev."

Boris was still hesitant, contemplating the idea and sounding negative. I tried to assuage whatever concerns he might have.

"It's a dangerous mission, man, no doubt about it, but maybe it's your time for glory. Lugansk is not Lugano. I don't want to add too much pathos, but someone has to save Ukraine and truly you strike me as one of the potential saviours at least of Lugansk."

To sound more humorous, friendly and sincere, I added, "If you perish fighting, my dear friend, I would pay huge alimony and child support for your dependents, but since you have none it mitigates my financial risks."

Boris laughed at that.

"You have a funny way of selling this idea, Misha. I think you are right though: you and me, and the support we have in Lugansk, it can be done."

I called Arthur into the room to deliver the final blow, which I hoped would be sufficient. I switched the phone to loudspeaker mode and turned to Arthur, so that Boris would hear on the other end.

"Arthur, in these turbulent times for our beloved Motherland, Boris has agreed to pick up the gauntlet and take a position as the governor of the embattled Lugansk district. Unfortunately whatever arms we were unable to sell over the years, the greedy and corrupt generals sold for themselves or maintained them poorly so they are near useless. So you might read somewhere about the Ukrainian army force being 100,000 strong, but realistically there may be only a few hundred really capable of fighting and even less properly equipped for the mission. Arthur, you should go out there for a few days to help Boris establish and begin enrolment of a new volunteer battalion, ready to fight for Ukraine, which I hereby call Lug. Form its backbone from our workers. Don't even try to object, it's an order this time."

This would be my almost official private army. As patriotic oligarchs were all financing troops, ammunition, purchase of military equipment or all of the above together, it felt right for me to get involved on a military level. My battalion, hardened in battle against separatists and Russians, would guarantee my security and dominance both from external aggression now and from possible internal encroachment later, if some people would have funny ideas after solidifying their grip over the country. This was a sort of neo-feudalism, as each oligarch patronised a certain area and cared for its self-defence from his own pocket. I had been bankrolling troops for years, ever since Gigo formed his protection squads, so I knew what had to be done and I had trained personnel for commanding positions.

Neither Arthur nor Boris tried to protest, so I assumed they weren't against the idea. I just wanted to make sure it would be for the right reasons.

"One more thing, bro, please rule as clean as possible. I don't want any stains smeared on your reputation and by virtue of our connection, spreading on to mine. You get a salary from me, so don't even bother to get extras on the side. That's important."

At this, he did protest though.

"Misha, what happened to you, man? If we undertake such an endeavour, we cannot miss the golden opportunity that comes with it, don't you see? It used to be a rich industrial region once."

I almost heard him drooling over the region's budget and other opportunities to promote our businesses or take those of competitors.

"Boris, the country has changed, but it needs to change more. You cannot apply the same techniques as before. Please, do as I say in the meantime and, believe me, I'll find a way to capitalise on our new position when the time comes. And by the way, please, consider not wearing that gold chain around your neck. This fashion is twenty years out of date already. You are going to be a politician, not a pimp, you got that?"

"Yes, Misha, I shall be upstanding and transparent." Boris huffed.

"Thank you, my friend. Ukraine will thank us one day. You might even get a statue erected."

"Yeah, yeah. Now you exaggerate."

"Too much? Okay. So I will call again soon, you can get in touch with Stepan and let him start dealing with the managers."

***

I should admit that Boris was probably born a great army leader, as he managed to hold on against several heavy attacks and flash mobs. It's a pity that it was too late for him to look into a career change. He managed to lead a decent resistance, although some of the district's areas and few towns were lost to the opposition.

One of Boris's many achievements made me particularly proud and excited. Boris called me up all upbeat, and reported that Lug, a battalion funded solely by me, had surrounded and then defeated, a notoriously vicious separatists' gang, headed by a ruthless commander nicknamed Kaleka, which means 'invalid' in Russian. This gang had been terrorising the region for over two months, and putting a stop to their raids and murderous antics was cause for celebration for the Lugansk people.

"You have heard this name, Kaleka?" Boris enthused.

"The name has come up in reports, but I don't know him," I answered truthfully.

"Then check this out, you're going to love it. I'm sending you his picture."

Hearing a beep, I opened the message application on my mobile phone and saw a small picture. It was obviously a dead body. I clicked on it and blew it up bigger.

"Is it? Yes! Yes, blyad, suka!" I screamed. Kaleka was my old friend Nazar. The corpse was clearly recognisable, although riddled with bullets.

"Got him, the motherfucker. Well done, Boris, you just made my day. You are my hero. Too bad you were born after World War II. If you were there you would capture the Reichstag much earlier than they managed without you."

But the daily reports weren't all good, all the time. A few days later, Boris called and this time I felt he was shaking on the other end of the line.

"Misha, I can't stand it anymore, man." Boris was on a verge of a nervous breakdown. "Do you remember Slavik, my nephew, who worked for us in Belarus a while ago?"

"Yeah. What's up with him?"

"He was watching some World Cup warm up match in a decent restaurant in Mariupol. Russia was playing yesterday. He and his friends are Ukrainian patriots, you know, so each goal the Russians conceded, they cheered. Anyway, just a few tables away there was another group - probably a Russian undercover unit. The third time the cheers erupted, this other group just started shooting at everybody in the place. Some of my nephew's friends were armed, so they returned fire. From what Slavik describes in a minute or two everyone was dead around him, while he was still struggling with his old jammed pistol, trying to make it shoot. He was so terrified and preoccupied that he didn't realise what had happened. So when all the shootings stopped, the place became silent all of a sudden, he stood up from behind the overturned table where he was hiding, and threw away his pistol in despair, thinking the Russian fuckers had already left. The impact fixed the weapon and it shot a bullet that smashed his left testicle."

It sounded harsh, but I stifled a laugh.

"Misha, after my brother died, he is my only living relative and he could've been killed there."

I thought I heard a muffled sob down the line. I didn't have much to say.

"Well, look at it from a different angle; he's got a lot of luck on his side, man, as he survived when everyone else died."

***

I will never forget the huge Soviet military parades on TV, broadcast every year from Moscow. All those vehicles carrying massive ballistic missiles and thousands of soldiers marching in Red Square. In my childhood, it was *Brezhnev*, the General Secretary, and his fellow senior leaders of the communist party that stood at the Lenin Mausoleum's tribune. With all their shiny regalia, they watched the impeccable order of the military show-off in front of them, under a huge banner with the portraits of Marx, Engels and Lenin. That was really impressive. So much power.

The same tradition was meticulously preserved by the Russians. This year's parade was especially menacing, as, I was sure it was intentionally designed to be. The endless lines of military machines: tanks, rocket launchers, air force fighters and others involved, were notably excessive. Although not officially proclaimed, the leitmotiv of the entire parade was to celebrate the annexation of Crimea and to emphasise the message that whoever defies Russia would have to deal with these stone-faced, well-trained and heavily armed soldiers. Maybe it was my imagination, but somehow I felt another unspoken message in the air - that the Russian military expansion was far from over just yet.

The TV cameras panned across the stage and focused on the Russian leaders supervising the parade beneath them, showing stern unsmiling faces one after another. Holy shit! The Puppet Master was second to the right from the president. Traditionally, the position on the tribune reflected the place in the political hierarchy. That was very, very concerning. It meant that my dear stepfather had moved up to the third or fourth position now.

After a few weeks of hearing Boris' daily reports on our forces successes in eliminating scores of terrorists only for their numbers to be constantly replenished from Russia, along with their arms' supply, I began to understand that there would be no easy victory. Being on the verge of defeat at some point, the separatists were quickly reinforced by Russian mercenaries and thousands of combatants of regular Russian army.

Although the defence minister - an old Puppet Master crony, was dead, still most of the Ukrainian military moves were leaked to the separatists. I wondered whether the entire staff at the army's headquarters was on a double Ukrainian-Russian payroll. These leaks from the army as well as from all other authorities made the life of the separatists much easier, as they could escape direct confrontation at ease and stage ambushes at will.

When the Russian regular army troops joined the fight, it became clear that the key to the problem was in Moscow. I tried to ignore this thought, but it was so obvious that it just kept haunting my mind. It was the Puppet Master who orchestrated the manoeuvres, tactics and strategy of the hostile troops in eastern parts of Ukraine, I had no doubt.

When Arthur returned to London, he confirmed my suspicions of the Russian role in the fighting. Separatists, wearing St. George's ribbons, were heavily supported by elite Russian troops often without insignia. Arthur used the trip to interrogate a few captive so-called terrorists. He reported back with a wry smile

"Russians invented this new type of undeclared war now labelled *hybrid invasion*. I've questioned a few obviously Russian soldiers, asking what Russian city they were from. They didn't want to confirm they were Russians and claimed to be individuals without citizenship as clearly instructed by Russian military intelligence. They were trying to be wise, you see. I had to become a bit physical and use new *hybrid* torture techniques to get all the details: their addresses in Russia, which platoon they belonged to, their orders, everything. They are completely brainwashed, sincerely thinking they are rescuing the Russian speaking population from Ukrainian nationalists threatening them."

Hearing that, I couldn't help asking: "Listen, Arthur, I wanted to ask you a while ago. You are born in Russia, your nationality is Russian, don't you feel a bit weird fighting and killing your own tribe?"

"Misha, you know me, I don't believe in ideals and all those compatriot notions. But as you asked, I treat Russians and

Ukrainians alike. We are the same people or very similar. Truly fraternal nations. We were closer than Basques and Spanish, Scots and English. I don't feel that Chechen or Tartar, who primarily volunteer to fight in Ukraine, is from my tribe just because they have Russian passports, any more than a Ukrainian guy who doesn't. The fact that some new napoleon in Moscow decided to use the army to open fire on our brothers in Ukraine, doesn't mean all Russians support him. Sowing hatred between Russians and Ukrainians is very dangerous. I'm afraid that territorial gains would be outweighed by external estrangement towards Russia and may even instigate internal unrest inside Russia, taking into account its complex multi-national and multi-religious population."

I was stunned. I'd expected a shrug, or a grunt at most.

"Wow, Arthur, I didn't expect such a deep and articulate analysis on your part. I see your point. You've actually given me an idea with your 'internal unrest' statement."

I suddenly understood that fighting them off, without dealing with their commander, wouldn't lead to any dramatic advantage and the entire area may boil with armed conflict for months, if not years. We needed to pull the strong popular support rug from under his feet.

Arriving at that conclusion, I tried to check whether the CIA would want to give me a helping hand in a small operation in Moscow. Romeo eagerly met me in London, all smug about his prophecies for Ukraine, but as soon as he heard about doing something in Moscow, all his smugness vanished. I didn't tell him exactly what was on my mind, but he didn't even want to hear about doing anything there.

"Listen, we condemn Russian aggression and publicly support the Ukrainian nation in fighting the perpetrators for its independence, but to stage a hostile operation in their capital? Forget it. No way, we couldn't do that, even if we believed it would be beneficial. We have the most pacifist government in years, Michael, and not less importantly - the most fragile economy since the Great Depression."

Cowards. I needed to count on just myself. I wanted to reactivate the plan B from Kazakhstan, which was for a bazooka assault on the Puppet Master's cortege in Astana, but I doubted that he would go there again given the war tensions, even if Aqsaqal invited him. I talked over the possibilities with Arthur, and he came up with his own plan.

After hearing the basic idea I was aghast.

"Arthur, it's not Poltava here we are talking about. We can't do anything of the same scale in Moscow."

"No, Misha, you didn't understand. In Moscow it's going to be only a prelude. The operation will take place at Sevastopol. We can induce the Puppet Master to pay a visit there."

Preparations

Surprisingly, the gathering in the conference room was quite large, with more people still arriving. We rented the room at the Wild Rose Bristol hotel, choosing this British city to be deliberately off centre, where we could organise adequate security and leave fewer possibilities for eavesdropping. As alternatives, London was too accessible and vulnerable to Russian clandestine agencies and Watford was too connected to me.

The city greeted us with rare sunny weather accompanied by a rather strong, but not too chilly to be unpleasant, wind from the sea, bringing along the aroma of salt and fish.

We managed to gather twenty five delegates: three from Ukraine, seventeen from Russia and another five from Crimea. Each was handpicked for sound reasons. The Russian opposition was so oppressed and demoralised that their spirit was low and, although many wanted it, only very few believed in the possibility of rocking the fearsome establishment, and even fewer were ready to give it a try. Having a number of likeminded compatriots around them would give them all a boost.

Most of the participants didn't know each other, while the celebrities were known to everyone. The Russian contingent consisted mostly of civilians, but included also a colonel of the FSB and an army general, whose participation was confidential and therefore they were hidden away in a separate room, wary of being seen by other delegates. They were adamant that we couldn't count on a military mutiny, and they wouldn't help us anyway with anything like that, but Arthur claimed that they both loathed the Puppet Master and all he represented, and for me that was good enough.

In regards to the colonel, Arthur elaborated that at one time he was on a par with Korablyov, considered one of the best KGB commanding officers, and they were both competing for the same promotion, but then Korablyov somehow managed to slander and defame him, so Korablyov was promoted and soon became a general, while our guest was derailed for years until he managed to clear his name and get his career back on track.

The army general, in a junior rank back then, commanded a USSR infantry platoon in Afghanistan while Korablyov was stationed there. As an honest Soviet officer, when he found out the atrocious and excessively cruel attitude of the Puppet Master towards the local population and prisoners of war, as well as his addiction to heavy drugs, he openly confronted Korablyov and threatened to report to Moscow on what was going on there. Soon, the general's wife was poisoned and died when she drank from a glass designated for the general. The blame was put on mujahedeen, but he was sure it was the Puppet Master. Before he retaliated though, his platoon was quickly recalled from duty and he was sent to serve at Kamchatka on the shores of the Pacific ocean - the farthest part of Russia. For a proud officer, veteran of fierce battles in that hostile land, and laden with medals received for his heroic performances in Afghanistan, an exile to Kamchatka was a slap in the face and no doubt it was at the Puppet Master's behest. Both Russian military men were perfect candidates for the task - the exact people I needed.

The non-military part was represented by a few famous bloggers, football ultra's, two oppositionists, two popular singers and an actor. The entire thing reminded me of the books about Russian nobility that emigrated after the communist putsch in 1917. The common denominator for all those present was their discontent with the current regime's policy and especially its aggressive stance concerning Ukraine.

As a simple admirer, I approached Igor Shutkov, a dinosaur of Russian rock, whose music I loved as a kid. He still looked fit and well, his hair still long, though thinning, and with an assortment of bracelets and chains as jewellery. I shook his hand, and said warmly: "Thanks for all the good music; I'm a big fan, Igor."

If Igor was my generation and older, beside him was a young guy wearing a baseball cap with a Che Guevara portrait on it. Hearing that he was being addressed as *Pandero*, I realised he was the famous rapper worshiped by the younger Russian generation. I hoped the Cuban revolutionist wasn't random on his cap, because I truly needed people with guts and balls.

Well, so far Boris, who promised a few celebrities in attendance, had kept his word. Some were still missing, but I decided to begin. The conversations died down. A technician somewhere behind the presidium where we were sitting tapped on the mike to make sure it was working; I unscrewed my water bottle, poured half a glass for myself and urged

Boris, sitting next to me, to take the podium and begin the meeting. At my prompting, Boris stood up, walked to the stage and cleared his throat. All eyes fell on him.

"Friends," he addressed the crowd with a winning smile. "Thank you all for coming. May our meeting bring new light to dark times. My good friend, Mikhail Vorotavich - politician, successful businessman and philanthropist, adept at Russian-Ukrainian fraternity will begin proceedings."

Boris stepped down, inviting me cordially to occupy the orator's tribune. Most attendees were all self-sustainable, famous and influential people, that's why spreading some non-reliable, propagandistic bullshit wasn't wise, so I kept to the facts and hoped they would suffice. Although adhering to a sincere approach, I couldn't avoid slogans completely.

"Dear guests. Thank you all for coming. I appreciate it would be quite difficult to keep this meeting under the radar, and so I thank you all for your courage and for your willingness to risk personal safety for the wellbeing of our proud nations. You came all this way because you care about the future of your countries and you are not happy with what's going on there. Since when did our countries, and I mean Russia and Ukraine, consider each other enemies? How did irresponsible warmongers sow the seeds of hatred and distrust between such fraternal nations? I myself was born in Ukraine, but the Russian language is my mother's tongue. I had family in Saint Petersburg. In my worst nightmare I couldn't have imagined Russian tanks crossing over into Ukraine with the purpose to conquer, to kill, to run over. I know that all of you share the same values that our nations, living alongside in their sovereign and integral states will always remain fraternal, and no politician or military strategist would drive a wedge between us. Now, I've invited here the people from Crimea, recently illegally adjoined to Russia. Mr Uralski here is the governor of Lugansk district, and he can share with us the most recent events and concerns from this territory. I know that many of you don't agree with the current situation, and voice your opinion, trying to persuade people to consider an alternative view. Unfortunately, many, both in Russia and Ukraine believe the propaganda broadcasts of the state Russian TV, therefore, I thought that if we want to achieve what we all strive for, we need to act in unison, to coordinate our efforts, otherwise each of us alone won't be able to pose any real opposition to the gigantic state apparatus of Russian government."

I paused after such a long monologue and took a sip of water, all the while studying the faces in front of me, who were all giving me their full attention.

"I offer three key points or elements that I believe that together we can achieve: to implement a series of concerted actions aimed at challenging the current aggression and escalation, to convince supporters and sympathisers to join our circle through a simple process of enrolment, and finally to offer adherence to the fundamental principle of equal fraternal nations and rejection of violence between brothers."

There were a few nods and scarce applause, but I didn't expect more than that. The main point was that the delegates seemed receptive and supportive.

"Now, Mr Boris Uralski will report on the current situation," I beamed, playing the politician.

Boris was less politically correct and more assertive. He described the unbearable conditions of the local population, who were suffering the most because of the armed conflict. He spoke of Russian mercenaries being recruited and sent to fight in Ukraine purely for money, were being captured regularly, and how both countries were suffering politically and economically.

"Who benefits from this enmity? Probably only the Americans, who are interested in weakening our countries," Boris added in conclusion.

When planning our speeches together, we had hesitated whether or not to raise this final point of contention, but decided it was a good idea, since having a third party antagonist could be a uniting element. We wanted to project a patriotic message not just one of traitors or conspirators.

There were a few grunts at the last section, old habits die hard, and America had been seen as an enemy for so many decades it was an easy target to direct enmity towards.

Boris stepped down to light polite clapping, and discussions between the delegates began around the table. Leaving Boris to keep an eye on things, which given that we could all be fairly hot-headed characters wasn't necessarily going to be an easy task, I thought I should go and have a word with the officers next door. The civilian demonstrations, protest marches and internet blogs weren't really my cup of tea anyway. Possible military involvement held more interest for me, given my recent troubles.

So, I grabbed Arthur and we moved to the smaller room, which Arthur checked several times for any alien devices. It was equipped with everything we needed: a table for ten with comfortable chairs and a big white board with five markers attached to it by the magnetic holder. A stock of plain white paper and some pencils were arranged in the middle of the table. I'd kindly asked everyone to leave all mobile phones with my assistant and after light refreshments and coffee were served, we were ready for what I saw as the main event.

Arthur stood at the head of the table and introduced everyone formally. I was delighted to see that both General Serebrov and Colonel Shatskikh had attended as promised. Arthur stepped aside, and I opened the discussions.

"Gentlemen, I am sorry to keep you waiting," I offered as an opening line. "Our other guests have been instructed on the true nature of the situation, and are now discussing how best they can all get involved. I am pleased to say there appears to be a positive vibe in the room."

The nodding heads acknowledged this, but barely a muscle moved on the line of stony faces.

"I didn't want to bore you with the pointless civilian palaver, gentlemen, I hope we can use this time for planning a more direct solution to our shared problem. I don't want to pry, but Arthur has told me in general terms, that you too have your own long histories with Korablyov. I hope that I'm among friends and there is nothing to be shy about, so I'll tell you what my reasons for getting squared with him are. And generally, it has nothing to do with Russian - Ukrainian tensions."

I told them Sara's story. Mostly facts, these weren't men that were interested in emotions. Shatskikh nodded and said that he had heard about this incident. It was important. I wanted them to understand that I was being sincere with them.

I told them about the assassinations attempts both in Kiev and in Watford, the hit squad in Tel Aviv and the torpedo in the Med. They sat and listened to my recent troubles without barging in or expressing anything. Remarkable military discipline. This was nothing like my chief-of-staff meetings with Boris and David, who never gave me a chance to say more than two sentences without interrupting me, usually with some silly joke. I didn't want to tire them with a long speech, so I made my last point.

"The Puppet Master and Russia are not at all synonymous. The dangerous game that the Puppet Master started is equally ruinous for Russia, as it is for Ukraine. I can't understand how he's been given such a free hand and the support of the Russian establishment. The Russian economy is already being affected by the sanctions and the farther the Puppet Master plans to expand, the more severe the sanctions will be. And believe me, once he finishes with those he considers as external enemies, he would turn to his internal ones, as his type cannot live without enemies. His life then doesn't have meaning. I am sure that you gentlemen understand this better than we do."

When I concluded, Serebrov, the General, reacted first.

"I want that junkie dolboyob dead. If you have a plan, I would like to hear it. You know that there is a price tag on your scalp, right?"

I turned to Arthur, puzzled by this last statement.

"Did you tell them?"

Arthur shook his head negatively. I never doubted him, so I continued.

"Well, you must be telepathic, General, because that's exactly the plan we have come up with. You are going to capture me and claim the bounty from our dear friend the Puppet Master."

That stunned them, without a doubt.

"Well, gentlemen, we need to have some bait that would be attractive enough for this motherfucker to swallow and it's just a matter of time anyway before he gets to me. My likelihood of surviving another assassination attempt is next to zero, so I have decided to be proactive. So, what we have conceived is that you, General, capture me and you, Colonel, make sure this news reaches the Puppet Master's table immediately."

"But how will that help? My soldiers will never turn on an officer."

"I understand that, General, except your soldiers will be substituted for mine just for the mission."

They were too struck to react at first, letting the idea roll around their minds before questioning it. Availing them of some more time, I continued with my explanations.

"I want to be completely honest with you all. This is a very risky operation. If you are caught collaborating with me, you'll be court marshalled and accused of the most grave felonies of the military code, so you should make a decision whether it's important enough for you to personally get involved. Don't do it for me. No reward that I can pay you, and I *can* pay, is worth doing it. Only if you care about the future of your country and your own score to settle, should you even contemplate participating in the operation."

222

The military men looked uneasy. And rightly so, as an unsuccessful mission would likely lead to treason charges and certain death. They huddled together; I sat back and waited for the next play. Only a couple of minutes passed, and the whispering stopped. Shatskikh stood and walked to the head of the table. I stood, my heart beating ten to the dozen in anticipation. If they were onboard, we had a chance. If not, I was probably living on borrowed time.

Shatskikh faced me, still straight-faced and impossible to read. He extended his hand, and grasped mine firmly when I extended it.

"I'm in," was all he said.

Serebrov was a little more hesitant, in keeping with the profile that Arthur had drawn up on him that stated that he was a more direct and conservative man. He asked a few more questions and after verifying that we really had thought through most of the details, he shook my hand too.

"Gentlemen, I am pleased that you see the benefits of my plan. I propose a short break for lunch before we get down to the intimate details."

I left Arthur in the room and went back to check on Boris and our other guests. Entering the room, I was pleased to see everyone engaged in conversation, stacks of papers, plans and outlines covering the table, and several lists on the whiteboard. Everyone appeared enthusiastic and ready to act.

"How was it?" Boris asked.

"What do you think? They are in! We just need to go over the fine details, but they're in - I can't fucking believe it."

"Good news, Misha. You are ready to be captured, my friend? That's the part I don't like."

I let out a sigh.

"There is no other way."

I sent Boris out to organise the food for both rooms, I stayed and chatted with the big group until the waitresses came in, then excused myself and rejoined Shatskikh and Serebrov. Over the meal, we analysed all the risk factors, finalised a tentative hourly schedule, decided on back up and default routines, and came to the conclusion that although the chances for success existed, they were not very high. Fuck it, it didn't matter to me. I was a walking dead man while the Puppet Master was around, I was going to give it a shot anyway.

***

Once we had a plan, although it would be extremely dangerous for me, I felt strangely relaxed while working on its realisation. Like the condemned man on death row, fear and anticipation of a bad outcome were pointless wastes of energy and brainpower. Instead, I was focussed and in the zone.

Our first series of concerted public unrest manifestations, as decided at the meeting in the big room, exceeded even our most optimistic expectations. The numbers of people on the streets in thirteen cities, including Moscow and Saint Petersburg, were so high that the authorities decided against their violent dispersal this time, as opposed to anything staged previously without my coordination. So far this was just a peaceful march.

In the aftermath though, two of our Bristol guests were marked as illicit instigators, detained and interrogated. I was sure some connection to me would be raised during those not-so-pleasant procedures. Surprisingly, they were soon released, and warned to refrain from propagating any such protest ideas again, or else. I advised them to make this all public, using the power of social networking, to provoke further outrage.

The Russian counter was imminent. Every other day or so I was personally demonised by the Kremlin journalists. I envied their inventiveness, as in just a few days I was portrayed as the worst enemy of the Russian people, traitor to the true interests of the Ukrainian Russian speaking population, a piggish and greedy Jewish oligarch, antichrist, warmonger and the most evil incarnation of Satan on earth.

After the third public event in Russia, during which course the angry crowd occupied the FSB building in Yekaterinburg and demanded the end of tyranny and cessation of militant actions in Ukraine and when the enrolment to our internet brotherhood hit three hundred thousand, my CIA friends called asking for a meeting. I had an idea of what they wanted, but as usual they managed to surprise me.

Romeo and Ken turned up at my house in a white Transit van, with Watergate Plumbing Services on its side. You've gotta love the American tongue in cheek sense of humour. We sat in my office and they outlined the reason for their visit.

"We take our collective hats off, Mr Oligarch. Very impressive. We see that you've mastered the art of the manipulation of social media like a real expert. Since you turned down the governor's position in Ukraine, we may recommend that our president appoints you as the head of information technologies department in the US. Interested?"

Romeo was joking this time, meaning to show though that I had earned some respect.

I responded in the same playful way: "Sorry, guys. I just signed a contract with the FSB for the director's position. If you want to have my interest, aim higher both position and salary wise."

Soon enough though the conversation turned to its real purpose.

"You know, Michael, it's a very interesting enterprise that you've launched there. I mean this brotherhood thing. Although you use it for political needs, it has become surprisingly viral, showing a remarkable exponential growth rate. You know our experts estimate that these things are worth money. Some serious money, actually."

"Romeo, I appreciate your courting and compliments, but I'm not selling anything at this point," I said firmly.

"Tell you what, Misha," he switched to Russian. "I'll give your mobile phone number, if you don't mind, to one very interesting lady. Her name is Juliette, in its French adaptation. It will be easy for you to remember: Romeo and Juliet. Meet with her and I'm sure you won't regret it."

Have they decided to seduce me after all? I pictured in my head the girl that waited for me in the American embassy in Bratislava. Yeah, I would do her eagerly.

"Sure, guys. I rarely turn down meetings with interesting ladies." I agreed and forgot everything about it until I received a call a few days later.

Fairies really do exist!

I didn't like calls from unidentified numbers, but I answered anyway, not expecting anything good considering recent events, and the battering my good name was taking on a daily basis.

"Hello, Michael? My name is Juliette and I was told that you might want to have an appointment."

I heard the voice of a very old lady with a distinct aristocratic accent. Although English wasn't my native tongue, I was quite au fait with regional differences. I imagined someone like Margaret Thatcher or Queen Elisabeth on the other end to connect the image with the voice.

"Err...an appointment?"

Then I recalled what Romeo had told me about his mythological lover.

"Ah, Juliette, right, of course. Where do you want to meet?"

She laughed mildly from my apparent change from incomprehension to recognition, or maybe from my slightly vulgar approach.

"Would London be good?"

"Just perfect."

I didn't believe that this 'Juliette' or anyone else could really help with anything, but I was curious as to why the CIA thought I would want to meet up with her. She gave me an address, which didn't ring any bells and we set the meeting for the next day at five o'clock.

Intending to be on time, I was ready to head out an hour before the meeting, but when I gave the address to my driver, he told me that there was no point in leaving just yet, as it was only fifteen minutes away by foot. I returned to my study and paced up and down, gagging to satisfy my growing curiosity at this imminent meeting. Half an hour passed, and I called for the driver again. I couldn't wait any longer.

My driver stopped by a highly decorated, ornate metal gate with cameras above and a built-in intercom. It didn't bear any sign, surname or number. The gate formed an organic extension to the high brick wall which surrounded the property, separating or protecting the inhabitants from the outside world. I rang the intercom and the gate started to open slowly. Someone must have been monitoring the gate camera.

The gate concealed a rather large mansion, built in a stunning renaissance style. Taking a look at a generous lawn in front of the building and the spacious garden with fountains and pedantically tidy lanes bordering each side, coupled with the location of the property, I guessed its value was considerably more than my own house, and mine definitely wasn't a cheapie.

I walked through the gate towards the house, where a uniformed valet greeted me at the door. I could swear that he expected me to hand him a walking stick and a top hat, but after a brief pause seeing that I had nothing to turn in, he ushered me into the dining hall, which was large enough to easily accommodate a United Nations General Assembly.

The valet moved the massive wooden chair back so I could sit down comfortably, and I was left alone. I looked around at the old paintings on the wall. All of them were portraits: some presented nobility with all the ribbons and orders around their neck and funny archaic haircuts and wigs, others strangely portrayed some orthodox Jews with sidelocks and kippah. What a strange mix.

Before I had time to muse over such an unusual collection, I heard the footsteps of someone descending the marble stairs leading from the upper floors at the far end of the huge hall. Seeing two elevators there, I wondered why someone would prefer to use the stairs.

An old lady, dressed in an old fashioned but rich style, judging from the huge diamond diadem around her neck, approached confidently and extended her hand to me. She probably chose the stairs to demonstrate that she was still fit despite her advancing age.

I stood up, not knowing whether she expected a kiss or a handshake, so I did both! First I shook it and then brought the hand to my lips. She smiled, seeing how awkward I was at ceremonial things. For some reason, memories of how Yuri Gagarin had an audience with the Queen of England and broke most of the etiquette rules suddenly jumped into my head.

"Viscountess Greenberg," she said solemnly. Her aristocracy was intrinsic, bred by generations. "But you can call me Juliette, young man."

Jewish nobility? This is something rare. The only one that I could think of was Baron Rothschild. I introduced myself, settling on Michael instead of Misha.

Reading the acute curiosity in my eyes, Juliette began to explain why she had called me.

"You might not know much about our dynasty, Michael, and it wouldn't be polite and modest to tire you with the details. What probably would be of some interest to you is that our family was one of the five members of the London Gold Fix for many decades."

Holy shit. I didn't say it loud. She wasn't just another rich old bag, for sure. These people controlled the global economy, fixing the global gold prices for years! I understood now, that she must've been one of those dynasties that made their fortunes in previous centuries. I probably had my mouth open in surprise, as Juliette's smile became even broader.

"Oh, Madam. This tells me a lot. I thought the members were almost legendary until now when I see that you are indeed, flesh and blood."

She had my attention alright and Romeo was right tagging her as an *interesting lady*.

"Michael, the reason that I've suggested that we meet, is actually concerning a business offer that I have for you. I know you are a very busy person, especially these days."

Even if she was being sarcastic, it didn't show. I liked business offers from serious people, so I was all ears.

"I think that you are aware that the global economy is not quite what it is perceived to be. The wealth is, and industries still are, too concentrated and although competition is declared and is absolutely wonderful to my liking too, not all areas are truly competitive."

Tell me about it! I was worth over forty billion dollars before the recent depletion of my assets, and I didn't have to compete for a minute with anyone in any industry in a normal sense of the word. Yeah, I competed sometimes in giving the higher bribe or offering a higher kickback, but once such *bidding* was decided, we usually coordinated with other significant players on the same market to decide what would be the prices and which market share and geographical district each would have. If it so happened that we didn't manage to come to a consensus, then a shooting competition would usually ensue. Nothing was left for the best man to win through business outmanoeuvring. I wasn't naive to think that only Ukraine was so unique.

"We decided to de-monopolise some of the areas where we have been active for centuries. Although you see a very old lady in front of you, our family has decided to turn to more innovative industries and to diminish our holdings in traditional business, just like Rothschild's formally withdrew from gold trading. In this line, we are investing massively in social networks and information technologies. Your emerging network, I don't know whether you view it as such, especially taking into account that it encompasses mostly dissidents in Russia, is of interest to us."

Not only to you, as Romeo and his CIA were also testing the waters. I was sitting, listening without interrupting for more than ten minutes. That was probably a personal record.

"I'm almost finished," Juliette stated, seeing that I was a bit fidgety, "So coming to the point, I thought to myself what can I offer you instead, and I just came up with a strange but it seems legal and logical idea."

She wasn't smiling anymore.

"At some point when the Soviet Union collapsed we thought we could integrate the Russian economy into the global one, so we partnered freely with Russian entrepreneurs and invested in Russian assets. Some think that it was a mistake, too big a bite to swallow, and that's obviously an arguable point. It so happens that our family bank serves as the custodian of the 20% share of Gazdiesel, which is registered under the name of Mr Alexander Korablyov. I can't tell whether he's the ultimate beneficiary or just the front for someone, but we can regard the documents as they are, at face value. Taking into account that Mr Korablyov is about my age, we cannot help but be concerned about his heirs and luckily for you, the information we have received is that your wife might legally claim this dubious honour."

Fuck me. She's well informed.

"If you would care to provide some proof, when the time comes, I can assure you, that we as the custodians and the owner of another 20%, will embrace you as a lawful partner."

That was a most bizarre offer, but, boy, what a sweetener it was. Gazdiesel was the second largest Russian oil exploration company with huge reserves of unexplored oil fields. Calculating quickly in my head, it was at least sixteen billion US dollars worth at face value. Gazdiesel was valued low at around eighty billion dollars, because of Russia's economical hardships and sanctions, but its true value was much higher than that, I didn't have the slightest doubt. This old lady here, had just offered to realise my dream of topping the Forbes wealthiest list!

How did she know that I was going to shorten the Puppet Master's natural aging? How come they know about Masha? I doubted that she worked for the CIA, but that they might've worked for her didn't sound quite so absurd to me.

"Ms Juliette, it's so kind of you to think of our heritage. You probably know my answer. Of course, I agree and I will see whether I can procure some proof. It's a done, albeit contingent, deal between us."

"Nice to do business with you, Mr Michael," she parodied me. "Of course, I wish Mr Korablyov a long and happy life. He's our valuable client."

Yeah, right.

"Thank you, Madam."

She gave me her business card, so I could contact her if necessary and invite her to the Puppet Master's funeral. I might've forgotten, but money was my main driver for so many years. Now, along with personal revenge, the Puppet Master's demise could bring me another sixteen billion dollars. But to get him I needed to risk my life. I wondered how Arthur ever agreed to the plan that we were about to set in motion.

Mortal Showdown

Our men started to trickle into the peninsula a few days in advance. It was going to be an all-out assault, so we needed as much manpower, firepower and hopefully luck-power as we could possibly accumulate.

My opening gambit of stirring up the Russian population against the regime was beyond successful, as the regime was really rocked and threatened by ever growing waves of popular public unrest. I hoped that soon their hands would be so tied up concentrating on saving their own lives and grip on power, they would leave Ukraine alone. But as long as the Puppet Master was alive and orchestrating the Ukrainian onslaught, that may never happen.

I landed at Simferopol, flying an indirect route through Baku, and presented a forged Russian passport to immigration, issued in the name of Fyodor Kondratov, registered at Rostov, the Russian Federation. I passed through border control with barely a second glance and thought things were going smoothly.

Just as I was exiting the outdated, provincial airport building, two men in civilian dress grabbed my arms from both sides, while another man, who lingered behind in the shadows came close and said: "You come with us. Don't do anything stupid."

I was supposed to get to Sevastopol unhindered! What the fuck had just happened? I was covered in a cold sweat, not knowing what to do. I hoped that Arthur's men were nearby and had spotted that I was being apprehended.

They led me to a black Audi with tinted windows, whose motor was already running. The two men who were holding my arms pushed me inside and then occupied seats on either side of me, while the man who'd told me not to be stupid, took the passenger seat next to the driver.

As the Audi sped off, the superior raised his sunglasses, turned to me and ordered that I hand over my mobile phone, documents and all other belongings. I looked back, no other car had scrambled in pursuit of us. The passenger leafed through my Russian passport.

"Kondratov, huh?" He laughed loudly and tossed my forged passport into the footwell in disdain.

The rest of the ride continued in total silence and lasted almost two hours. Either the car's air-conditioner or the deodorant of those seated beside me wasn't strong enough, because the stench of sweat became totally unbearable after the first twenty minutes. If anyone farted on top of that, I was sure we would've all collapsed unconscious from the poisonous gas. No one said a word, the driver didn't even put the radio on and not even one mobile telephone rang, including mine. It became obvious fairly quickly that the mission was official, as we never stopped at the traffic lights, using a police siren to warn other cars to stay back.

I read a city sign *Sevastopol* as we finally turned off the shabby highway. Another twenty minutes and the sea became visible in the distance and soon after we approached a huge bay full of military vessels. The tires screeched as the car came to a sudden halt in front of a building by the bay on which a huge sign read: "Command of the Russian Black Sea Military Fleet." Until that moment I had harboured a tiny hope that there was some kind of change in plans while I was on the flight from Baku and these were our people apprehending me to make it look realistic. Looking at the sign, my optimism was shattered.

I'm finished, I thought. I was in the wrong hands, as *my* general belonged to the Sevastopol military commandant office, completely unrelated to the navy.

My silent company led me up some stairs to the second floor and pushed me into an empty room with just a table in it and two chairs. They handcuffed me and left the room, locking it from the outside. I looked up - the window was barred.

Half an hour passed and I saw the light outside became dimmer. I started to panic. My handcuffed arms ached and, seeing as I wasn't connected to the chair, I considered passing my arms under my backside, through my legs and bringing my hands to the front. I decided against trying. No point antagonizing anyone further, and besides that - my aching arms were going to be the least of my worries if Arthur and his team didn't know where I was.

The sun went down fully and the room darkened in harmony with the outside. Terrible thoughts filled my head. Could I kill myself somehow? Anything to deny the Puppet Master the satisfaction of doing me in personally. Eventually I heard the key in the lock and looked to the door in nervous expectation.

The light flicked on and a naval officer wearing white dress uniform entered followed by his adjutant, equipped with a legal pad, some forms attached to it, pen and tape-recorder. Having no visible torture gear still meant they could use fists and legs for a good traditional beating.

"Ahh, dear Mr Kondratov-Vorotavich," the senior officer remarked, smiling smugly. At least he's an intelligent type, I thought. "What brings you here, except for my Audi? The summer recreation season is postponed this year, haven't you heard about it?"

"Officer, I'm an Israeli citizen on a business tour. I can't understand who owns jurisdiction over the Crimea peninsula, but both Russia and Ukraine have waived visa requirements for Israelis. Unless you are captain Nemo, wishing to offer me a ride on your submarine, you might proceed with pressing charges, if you have any, and call the Israeli consul to come visit me here."

"Ha, ha, ha. I thought that you might be a smart ass. Well, travelling with a counterfeit passport would be the minor of your offences, believe me. You will soon have someone pay you a visit. Not a consul though. Someone from Moscow is very excited about your sudden appearance here. So excited, that he will come visit you personally in order not to take any risks connected with your transportation to Moscow."

I didn't have anything to say to that, no smartass comments came to mind.

"You know what?" He turned to the adjutant. "Let's wait with the protocol for now, Lieutenant. Maybe it'll be better not to formalise his detainment just yet. I'm sure the bounty is mine anyway and probably the next rank," he added with that smug grin that was already starting to annoy me.

They turned to leave, but before exiting, the bastard said: "I am afraid our five-star hotels are currently overbooked, but we can extend our cordiality and accommodate you here. As you are probably accustomed to a guarded sleep, you'll feel right at home, knowing that the compound is guarded by a marine unit. Sweet dreams, Mr Vorotavich."

Some minutes later the door opened again, and someone tossed a bottle of water in without giving a second thought to how I was supposed to drink with my hands handcuffed behind my back. At least an hour passed without any more visitors, so I shuffled my arms underneath me, afraid of getting stuck in this awkward position, but managed to wriggle until my arms were in front of me. Now I could open the flask and whet my parched mouth. I was under no illusions as to who the guest coming from Moscow was, as my bait status had worked perfectly. Unfortunately, this was the only part of my plan that had worked, and so I had no reason to look forward to meeting him under such circumstances.

***

The night I spent at the Russian Black Sea Fleet Command was the worst of my life. I would happily trade it for another coma of any duration. Death would also have been a good trade off. It wasn't so much the circumstances - just the anticipation of the Puppet Master's triumphant arrival that ate me from inside. I wasn't afraid of dying so much, as I was already accustomed to the idea; it was being so defeated that agonised me. All my efforts and achievements seemed to be rendered insignificant now.

This would be my last day, I thought. That's not how I figured it would be. I didn't expect to die like a Roman senator with a glass of wine in a pool, surrounded by beautiful women and an orchestra playing, although it would be nice. I was prepared for a car bomb, a bullet or a stab to finally take me down. Being imprisoned and then executed was probably the worst scenario I could think of.

Strangely, as the morning prevailed over the night, and the sun began to peek over the horizon, I became more relieved, almost at peace. Today everything would come to an end. I wouldn't have to worry anymore about the Belarus project, Ukrainian war, or Russian uprising. My wife and kids would be well off even without me. I wasn't with them much these days anyway and just provided their finances, of which they would still have more than enough. I heard voices in the corridor and stepped inside the handcuffs as quickly as I could, so that my arms were behind me again.

The Puppet Master entered alone, smiling, maybe for the first time in many years, and locked the door behind him. If any guards accompanied him, they were left outside the cell. I eagerly returned his smile. I'm positive that he didn't expect to find me in such an elated state of mind but it didn't show on his face.

He quietly took the second chair. An unknowing bystander, seeing us smiling to each other would imagine a father and son meeting up after a long time apart. To some degree, this is what it was.

"Misha, Misha, Misha," he finally spoke. "There were so many troubles with you. How many times you've escaped my traps. Thrice I've arranged for you to bid this world goodbye, but you came out alive somehow and that without even counting the failed attempt to blast you at your stadium. And even the Chechens failed with their own attempt. What are you, a salamander, coming unscathed from the flames? Too bad you've chosen greed for your life's purpose, as you could've been a good soldier of communism. I was prepared for any eventuality, except for this one, that you would come straight into my hands, dear. What a nice surprise. What brings you here, Misha?"

The Puppet Master was obviously in no hurry, enjoying this conversation with his helpless prey.

"I thought you knew," I chided in response."To meet you, of course. Stop this farce, you old fart. What have *you* chosen? Some ephemeral idea that is long dead. Forget about communism, it doesn't work, as long as there are not enough Mercedes for everyone. And you can't have them common, as everybody wants his own and of the most prestigious model no less. Besides, what about this 20% stake in Gazdiesel I hear about? Is that not greed, huh? Is it a charity? Give me a break."

I laughed angrily at his face.

"Oh, you know even that, my dear Misha. But it's not what you think it is. I've taken it for myself to preserve it from being sold or stolen by greedy politicians like you and when I would reinstate the rule based on just and fair ideology, it will return to the Russian people," the Puppet Master uttered solemnly.

"Yeah, right. A butcher like you cannot build or reinstate any just rule. No way. Sell it to someone else. And anyhow, when were you thinking of doing it? What, you've found a potion of immortality, old man? You are dead in a year or two, that is unless I finish you off earlier. Too bad probably not from my hands though. When exactly did you plan to return it? Spare me this bullshit."

But the Puppet Master didn't seem to be moved by my profanity.

"Mishenka, it'll happen much sooner than you think. Let me finish my little game here to join Ukraine, after which Belarus will follow, no doubt about that. Maybe I still have a few years to expand it even beyond that. I personally fancy Poland and Slovakia as good republics for my little project of rebuilding a Slavic empire, which, if you ask me, should stretch from the Atlantic to the Pacific. How does Paris oblast sound to you? You probably prefer London autonomous district, don't you? Although not Slavic, we can let some other nations join it. And I have some ideas on how to adjust the governance in our glorious country, so that we would eradicate this foul capitalist influence."

"You are a megalomaniac, you know that? Tell me the Scotland independence vote was also your idea" I smiled contemptuously. I didn't believe that any of what he said was possible.

"It's undoable and I already proved it to you. Do you think this uprising in Russia is just the work of foreign intelligence, as you try to present it in your controlled media? Of course, not. People are truly tired of tyranny and oppression, and I just helped them to find who is responsible. Yes, they don't like rich people like me and I agree that it's not fair that I control the factories built long ago by their fathers and grandfathers, acquiring them for peanuts, but there isn't any better governance than capitalism. It reflects natural instinct: to be first, to succeed. You can't preach equality, when it's not implementable. Not enough choppers for every fucker, do you understand or not? Capitalism is the same as primitive society - the strongest rules, only we amended it a bit, so the strength is measured in money. You can't subordinate free people of the new internet era if they oppose it and, believe me, they do. You may tactically succeed here and there, but your ultimate failure is inevitable."

"Mishenka, you are an imbecile, unfortunately, but I would cleanse this world from a mental type like you. If you want to understand before you die, I'll explain it to you. You think that what's good for Jan or John is equally good for Ivan and Dima? But that's exactly where your mistake is. These lousy foreigners can curse their governments, but still cherish some inexistent European values, work hard, sweat, take risks, hoping that one day they would win the race and become rich, whereas Slavs have a different mentality. If you don't force them to do something, most would drink and lie in a hammock or revert to violence. European Africa to simplify it for you. You can't leave them on their own; it's not in their genes. You have to reign them hard and foster their pride. That's the right formula..."

I was tired of his shit already. We could trade barbs and insults for hours, and still I would be dead by the end of the day.

"Enough of your bullshit. I can only take so much. I'm tired of talking with a fool. I hope that there are disillusioned minds in Russia who can promote a more realistic agenda. Do what you must and get it over with."

"Pah, you give up already? You weak, pathetic fool of a man." He spat. "I thought we could have a nice conversation, but it seems you are ready to be punished."

The Puppet Master unclipped the catch on his belt and took out the vintage NR-40 combat knife he still wore. He leaned forward and spoke as if in awe of the cold steel.

"Can you guess how many people's blood has been spilt by this?" He asked, admiring the dagger. "I couldn't remember, you know. But still, I think this one will be the most satisfying."

I was stiff, coiled like a spring, ready for any opportunity to attack the Puppet Master if the chance arose. He sat in front of me, smiling his stupid grin as he fingered the weapon. The bastard was enjoying himself, and soon he would start carving me up.

From nowhere, a series of blasts rocked the building. The lights went out and alarms started to ring. This was my chance – don't think, act!

I sprung forward with all my strength, overturning the table separating us with my knees and using the element of surprise and superior weight to force the Puppet Master back in his chair. He toppled backwards, and in that split second I frantically struggled to get my hands in front of me. Puppet Master got to his feet just as I managed to do so, and he leapt at me. Elderly or not, he was still an apt killer. I twisted sideways, rolling with his body weight and landed on top of him, striking two hard double-handed blows to the jaw. He bucked and threw me off, and went for his knife which had scuttled into the corner.

I went after him, my fight or flight reflex urging me to do the former. As he turned, the knife held towards me, I made a grab for it, getting a hold on the hilt. We struggled, and I head butted the bastard on the nose, splintering it and causing blood to gush out immediately. The Puppet Master shrieked, and in that instant I leaned into him, kneed him in the groin and managed to twist the blade away from me and into the Puppet Master's shoulder. I ground the blade deep into the muscle, twisting it and enjoying the bulging eyes response it invoked in my archenemy.

The Puppet Master's efforts were concentrated on pulling the knife from his shoulder, so I went for his throat, jabbing the tips of my fingers into where I hoped the cricoid cartilage was located. He coughed, started gagging, and his hand came off the knife and tried desperately to strip my hands away. I was a man possessed, and it was an impossible task for the old man. He aimed a series of strikes at the side of my head, using the heel of his hand, but in his weakened state, and with my rage, I barely flinched. He returned to trying to get my hands from around his throat, but it was pointless. His arm dropped, and I watched as the last flicker of life disappeared from his cold, grey eyes, enjoying his agony.

I squeezed for what seemed like another minute, then let go. The Puppet Master's body slumped to the ground like a bag of rags.

"Blyad suka. See you in hell," I said to the corpse. With this motherfucker dead, the guards could enter and kill me now, I didn't mind. I smiled broadly enjoying this rare and possibly last moment of glory.

I tentatively approached the door to listen for the guards, but as I leant forward to put my ear to the steel it exploded from a limited local blast, knocking me backwards. I laid there, stunned, and blinked as shadowy figures entered the room.

"Misha?" A friendly voice called out.

"Arthur, you son of a bitch. About fucking time."

Arthur appeared through the smoke, and crouched down to help me to my feet. Once upright, Arthur saw the lifeless body of the Puppet Master, his dead eyes staring into nothingness.

"So, my champion prevails. I would have liked to have seen for myself."

"Handcuffs!" I screamed, wanting to be free of my shackles and eager to escape from the cell.

Arthur held my arms out, and angled a shot at the metal chain so that the bullet would continue its trajectory into the fallen Puppet Master.

"We don't want to go through all this to be taken out by a ricochet, huh?"

Arthur fired, and I was free. My fists were numb, my fingers ached from the pressure I'd exerted on the Puppet Master's throat. I looked down at my fallen enemy and used my leg to turn his face to us.

"He looks...unhappy," Arthur mused.

"You're a fucking comedian today, Arthur. I prefer when you keep fucking silent. Chop off his hand and take some blood from his wounds and let's get out of here."

"Yes boss."

Even if he was startled for a second by these strange orders, Arthur took his knife out and did as he was asked without explanation.

"And take some pictures of his face and body."

I needed the Puppet Master's DNA, not knowing which tissue was exactly needed, so taking a hand and some blood seemed like a good idea.

***

We exited the compound with Arthur clutching the Puppet Master's hand like a grotesque souvenir, and another squad member holding the water flask that I'd struggled to drink from the night before, now filled with his blood. Ten masked and heavily armed men waited outside the building.

Arthur led the team to a group of amphibious vehicles parked by the entrance, all bearing Russian military markings. General Serebrov waited by the vehicles and saluted me as I approached.

"Well done." The General congratulated, and extended his hand.

Offering my hand with the remains of the handcuffs hanging like bracelets, I smiled broadly and countered.

"I thought you would never come."

"We were a little delayed, Misha, but I always keep my promises."

"I never doubted you, General, but it was a bit close for comfort."

"I assume my old comrade is no longer with us?" Serebrov asked.

I turned to Arthur, who held up the bloody souvenir.

The General shook his head in disgust.

"I don't even want to know," he scoffed. "We should leave now, before reports of explosions here reach unfriendly ears."

"Yes, General. I would like to get far away from here. What about the sailors?"

"They are locked in a warehouse. They suffered no casualties, as they weren't expecting seemingly Russian soldiers to turn on them, so we subdued them easily. They have no idea about the high-ranking visitor. We will phone the police when we are well clear and tell them to free the men."

"And the security men who took me at the airport, what about them?"

"No idea. Maybe they were the ones who put up a fight when we started to comb the building, maybe not. A few are dead, as you can see. Either way, they will scurry off like rats now their leader is gone. They will say nothing, you can be certain. They failed to protect their master, they won't broadcast that without putting themselves in mortal danger."

"Good to hear. So the Puppet Master just...disappears."

"It might appear so. Shatskikh may help it look that way. Come, we should get far away from here. Men!" The General commanded. "Start your engines."

We jumped in the vehicles and headed away from the naval base. I told Arthur to stop near a restaurant about ten kilometres away, whose owner was terrified seeing four amphibious military vehicles pulling into his parking area. I sent Arthur inside to get some ice for the hand and to pack around the flask of blood. We were mobile again in minutes, and I sat in the back of one of the vehicles, next to Arthur.

"Where were your people, Arthur? How did you let them apprehend me?"

"I had a crew waiting for your arrival, but purely by accident one of my men popped up as a match on the FSB airport monitor. They detained my crew, but couldn't squeeze from them anything more than your expected arrival, because they didn't know more than that. Shatskikh informed me right away and advised that the news had already reached Moscow, but it took time to come up with an alternative plan to rescue you from the naval command centre. Good that we had almost forty men ready for action and a real Russian army general to command them. It wasn't too hard to tie up those stupid sailors once we reached the navy base."

"Don't expect to get any commendations from me, Arthur," I tapped on his back lightly, appreciating that he had persevered and saved me after all. He finally looked somewhat relaxed.

"Can I go home now?" I asked his permission jokingly. "You don't need me for the Chechens, I hope."

A few hours later we crossed the peninsula into Ukraine, our way through cleared by General Serebrov who accompanied us all the way. We went straight to the medical laboratory in Nikolaev, already prepared for our arrival following my telephone instructions.

Epilogue

I called Juliette with my devastating news.

"Madam, I'm so sorry to inform you that your client has perished in a local military revolt. I extend my sincere condolences at his premature demise."

I hated all these lies but that's how it should've been said. I didn't think the etiquette of English nobility allowed me to call the fucker the names I preferred for his description. Equally, I couldn't say openly that I was so happy that he died. We set up a meeting in London to proceed with what we had discussed previously.

The formalities were simple, but the lawyers involved on both sides managed to end up with few hundred thousand pounds in fees anyway.

I assigned my Russian organisation to Juliette and presented the DNA test results together with the decision of the Ukrainian court that ruled - without too much monetary incentive - that Masha, my wife, was Korablyov's daughter and ordered a re-issued birth certificate for her.

Juliette handed over the papers that declared that my 20% stake of Gazdiesel was kept in the bank's custody to the favour of my family now with Masha being the prime beneficiary.

"Congratulations, young man, and please, pass my sympathy to your wife regarding her father."

Juliette managed to combine the countenance of pleasure from the successful closing of the transaction and the phoney sadness from Korablyov's death.

"By the way, once the Russian government becomes more favourable, I'm sure they will look into the issue of the assets that were nationalised or expropriated. I'm confident you might get your Crimean companies and assets returned."

I already had an idea who she was and it was clear, if she mentioned it, that the aforementioned change was imminent.

"I wouldn't be surprised to see your name on top of the Forbes list in the next edition, when Gazdiesel regains its true value. I'll have a word with the publisher to update him on our business transaction. He would appreciate being the first one to know."

Juliette smiled like a good fairy would after dispelling the charms of a vicious witch.

"Thank you, madam, err... your Excellency. I appreciate everything you have done. We'll be in touch then. Thanks for all the help."

I bowed slightly and went out to the street not afraid to walk home anymore, not expecting an assassin to appear from behind the hedges, or a car to pull up with masked gunmen spilling out ready to take me down.

My dream had come true, but it turned out to be somewhat hollow! I thought that first place would make me the winner and maybe technically I was. But what was it worth, if there were real rulers of the world above me, in the shadows, holding the real wealth and power. Were it not for their goodwill and consent I wouldn't have achieved the goal on my own.

Money had always been the prime motivator in my life, and I had learned that it didn't bring me happiness or peace of mind. Now I had achieved everything I had set out to do, I felt empty and disappointed. However, my next aspiration had become kinda obvious.

About the author

Nik Krasno was born in Kiev, USSR in the seventies. At the age of 17, seeing the enormous Soviet Empire crumbling around him, Nik immigrated to Israel, where he studied law in Tel Aviv University. He became a lawyer at the age of 23.

Returning to now independent Ukraine in the late nineties as an Israeli citizen, Nik established with partners an international law firm and managed it during its first years. He built the firm's reputation and later supervised its work from an Israeli law office. As a lawyer Nik counselled a wide range of multinational sovereign, corporate and individual clients, engaged in diverse areas and industries.

Nik holds an LLB degree from Israel and an LLM degree from Ukraine.

Simultaneously with promoting his law office, Nik worked for an international business group and took part in different projects primarily in real estate as well as in privatisation, defence, medicine and telecommunications in Ukraine and some other countries, such as Moldova, Russia, Poland and Lithuania. He has been sharing his time between family in Israel and work and business mostly in former USSR countries.

After selling his share in the law office, Nik currently resides and works as an independent legal practitioner and an author in Israel.

Nik is married + 4.

Acknowledgements

Many thanks to Carlito Sofer for some brilliant ideas, embodied in Book One, that I had an honour to develop further in this sequel, to David Thurlow for his thorough revision and editing, which contributed enormously, and to his wife for her encouraging feedback, to Ilanit Galam for another piece of marvellous design and to my family for their patience and support.